ESCAPE FROM THE ETERNAL FLAME

Yvi Valentin

Escape From The Eternal Flame

Copyright © 2017 by Yvi Valentin

ISBN: 1544076908

ISBN-13: 978-1544076904

"Better to die fighting for freedom than be a prisoner all the days of your life."

-Bob Marley

Chapter 1

The interrogation room was dimly lit and dreary with grey walls. Sitting at the old, cracked table were a man and woman. Tensions were high between the two. The woman confidently stared into the two way mirror. The man on the other hand, who was new to the facility, appeared confident but the woman in front of him could tell he was nervous.

"You saw the picture; now tell me what you know." He was irritated by her refusal to acknowledge him. "Alpha 411, I need an answer!"

"I have a name you know," she snapped.

"We don't use names in here."

Her frizzy blonde hair flew in her face as she yelled. "I know that, I've been here for five years!"

She immediately regained her composure. She calmly pulled her hair out of her face, revealing her sky blue eyes. Her flushed cheeks quickly returned to the same sickly pale tone as the rest of her skin.

"Then you should know the drill by now."

"You're the new guy so I'm going to let this one slide but after your boss gets here in a minute, you're going to find out exactly who you're dealing with."

"What's that supposed to mean?"

"It means I don't cooperate with you people. Not since the day I learned what's really going on in this hellhole."

"You have to tell me what you know," he said desperately.

"Your boss is about to walk through that door to tell you all about me."

The door opened and in walked an older man with noticeable wrinkles. Despite his skin being a subtle shade of orange and his slicked back salt and pepper hair, no one dared make fun of him. His permanently stern, green eyes made him intimidating to almost everyone in the facility. He was the one who could make

2

life in the facility even more of a nightmare for anyone he wanted.

"How did you know that?" he asked, stunned by her accuracy.

"Alpha 411, you can go back now."

"My name is Lottie!"

"Don't be ridiculous, your real name is Charlotte. Now it's time for you to leave."

Lottie slid her chair away from the table. "Be careful Timmy, your boss bites."

"How did you know my name?" The color drained from his usually pinkish face.

Only his wife ever called him Timmy. He much preferred Tim. He ran his fingers through his short brown hair as he thought about what happened between him and Lottie since he sat down. He realized he never mentioned his name. There was no way she could have known. He wiped the sweat from his brow and loosened his tie.

Tim's brown eyes locked onto Lottie as she smiled mischievously and left the interrogation room. "Jay, what just happened?"

Jay made sure Lottie wasn't outside listening in and closed the door. "That was Alpha 411. She is a highly skilled psychic we acquired."

Chapter 2

Lottie made her way into the cafeteria and took her seat at the table that had been hers for five years. She had no desire to eat; she only wanted to get out of this place.

"You're not eating again, Lottie?"

She looked up at those bright blue eyes and wavy red hair. "Matt, do we have to go through this every time?"

Matt placed his tray on the table across from Lottie and sat down. "Yes, you've been in here five years and I've had to force you to eat every day."

"I never asked you to do this for me."

"I know." He handed her half of his sloppily made peanut butter sandwich. "It's my responsibility to take care of you."

"No it's not," she argued. "You're just as trapped as I am."

"Yeah...well...I still care about you."

5

"Matt, we didn't know each other until we got here."

"What's your point?"

"You've been giving me half of your sandwiches since day one. There's no way you could have cared about me back then."

"I cared enough to not want you to starve that day."

"And every day after that," Lottie added.

She thought he was annoying at first because of his gentle nature and insistence on making sure she was healthy. But after everything they had been through together, she grew fond of Matt. She didn't want to let it show or the tyrants running the place would use it against her.

"Hi, do you mind if I sit here?"

A shaking girl stood to the left of Lottie. Her brown eyes filled with fear, fixed on the ground. Her tanned skin clean and smelling of rose scented soap and her curly, black hair neatly done told Matt and Lottie that the scared girl in front of them was new to the facility.

"You can sit next to me," Lottie answered.

"Are you new here?" Matt asked.

"Yes," the new girl nervously said.

"What's your name?" Lottie asked.

"Sophie."

"I'm Lottie, and this is Matt."

Sophie smiled weakly. "It's nice to meet you."

Matt nodded. "You too."

"You look so young," Lottie observed.

"I'm sixteen." Tears filled her eyes. "What is this place?"

"It doesn't have an official name but everyone who ends up here calls it the eternal flame," Matt answered.

"Why's that?"

"The eternal flame is known as the place where souls go to die," Lottie began. "Once a soul is destroyed in the eternal flame, it can never go back to what it once was. The same goes for this place. Once you get sent here, you can never go back to your old life."

"How long have you guys been here?"

"Five years," Matt and Lottie answered simultaneously.

"Why are they keeping us here?"

"The United States government has spent years trying to turn psychics into weapons," Matt explained.

"They've been using us for experiments," Lottie added. "And when they think someone is ready, they're forced into becoming soldiers."

"W-what kind of experiments do they do?" Sophie stammered.

Matt and Lottie stared at each other, wondering if they should tell Sophie the truth. After being imprisoned in the eternal flame for five years, they had seen it all. Some of it was gruesome and others were tame.

"What have you experienced so far?" Matt asked.

"I was questioned about what I did to land myself in here and then they asked me to prove I had the abilities I told them about," Sophie answered.

Lottie's face filled with concern. "Did you tell them about all of your abilities?"

"No, just the ones I'm good at."

"Don't tell them about the rest," Matt said.

A look of confusion spread across Sophie's face. "Why not?"

"If you want a chance of surviving this place, you have to keep secrets," Lottie whispered.

"Alpha 411!" a guard shouted. Lottie turned around to see what he wanted. "You're wanted in the Zulu Ward."

Lottie wasn't looking forward to going to the Zulu Ward. Her heart broke every time she was sent there. She tried to keep herself from crying. Anything that could be used against someone was used as much as possible to get them to break.

Matt held Lottie's hand as she mentally prepared herself for the trip. He felt sorry for her. He knew what a trip to the Zulu Ward did to her. He wanted to be able to do more to comfort Lottie but just about everything was banned from the eternal flame. Matt gave Lottie's hand one last squeeze as she stood up to leave.

"What's the Zulu Ward?" Sophie asked.

Chapter 3

"You told me to show her the picture and find out what she knows," Tim started. "You didn't say anything about her being psychic."

"This is a secret government facility," Jay pointed out. "Did you really think you would be told the whole truth?"

"Why is she so uncooperative?"

"No one knows. No one has been able to get a word out of her in years."

"She seemed pretty chatty to me."

"Yes, that was the first time she has said anything in this room but none of it was about what we need to know."

"How do we get her to cooperate?"

"We have our ways," Jay answered deviously.

"What are you going to do?" Tim felt the sweat dripping down his face. He never wanted anyone to get hurt. He wondered if he was right for the job. He contemplated quitting but there was part of him that felt the need to stick around to learn as much as he could about this nameless facility.

"There are certain buttons we can push to get her to crack but so far none of it has worked."

"Then how do you know it will work?"

"She has been here five years, she's bound to crack eventually."

"I need to know exactly what I'm dealing with if I'm going to get the necessary information out of her," Tim demanded.

"You need to know only what I tell you." Jay was so full of himself, completely in love with the authority he had over Tim.

"How do you expect me to find out what she knows without knowing everything about her?"

"You were brought here because you're the best interrogator in the country. Now I suggest you keep your questions about this place to a minimum."

"Understood."

"Alpha 411 was very willing to help us when she first got here. She got used to this place after six months and stopped cooperating. She hasn't said a word to anyone since then."

"Why do you think she chose to talk to me today?"

"She has the ability to see inside people's minds. She can read your thoughts and see all of your memories. She must have seen something she liked," Jay explained. "Come with me, I have something to show you."

"What is it?"

"It's Alpha 411's only weakness."

Chapter 4

Lottie took a deep breath as she entered the Zulu Ward. Part of her liked the visits but another part of her was always devastated by them. She knew what came after those visits and needed to prepare herself for it.

"Alpha 411, I'll take you to see Zulu 222," said a guard as Lottie came into view. He stared at Lottie expectantly. "Are you ever going to talk to me?" Lottie still didn't respond.

The guard shrugged as he gave up on trying to talk to Lottie and led her down the corridor. The walls and floors were concrete, just like every other part of the eternal flame. Lottie didn't like the color grey, she always found it depressing. Her nerves peaked as they stopped in front of a door with a sign saying: Z-222. She took a deep, calming breath.

"You have five minutes."

Lottie nodded. As much as she wanted to argue for more time, she didn't want to speak a word to that horrible man. She walked into the room and straight for the little girl. She wrapped her arms around the girl, unwilling to let go.

"Mommy, I can't play with my dollies like this."

"I'm sorry Emma, I'm just so happy to see you," Lottie said as she let go of her daughter.

Emma had the same wavy blonde hair and blue eyes as Lottie. Unlike Lottie, Emma's fair skin emitted a healthful glow. She was a sweet girl but it was best not to underestimate her ability.

"Have you seen daddy?" Emma asked.

"I was just eating lunch with him before I came here."

"He said I'm being sent to the Zulu Yankee Ward tomorrow."

"That's great sweetie!" It was bittersweet for Lottie. She was relieved Emma was able to move on to the next section but at the same time she didn't want her two year old daughter to be just as trapped as she was. "Are you nervous?"

"Yeah," Emma answered. "What if the other kids don't like me?"

Lottie kissed Emma's forehead. "They'll love you Ems, you're a great girl."

"Mommy, I saw something yesterday and daddy told me to only tell you."

"What was it?" Lottie's heart began racing. She knew it wasn't going to be good if Matt told Emma to keep a secret. They agreed when she was born not to allow her to keep any secrets until she was old enough to understand.

"I can show you." Emma stared directly into her mother's eyes and sent the vision to her.

Lottie saw herself tending a garden in the back yard of a house. She wasn't sure how, but somehow she knew this was her home. She watched Matt chase Emma around the yard as she giggled with delight.

Tears filled Lottie's eyes as she watched her family enjoy their freedom. She couldn't wait for that day. She hoped it would happen soon. The question remained: how were they going to escape?

Emma placed a hand on Lottie's shoulder. "Why are you crying mommy?"

Lottie wiped the tears from her eyes. "I'm just happy, sweetie. Your vision was beautiful but your daddy's right, you can't tell anyone about it."

"Why not?"

"Because Ems, if the wrong person finds out they'll make sure it doesn't happen," Lottie whispered.

"Good to see mother and daughter bonding," Jay said as he entered the room with Tim right behind him.

"Why can't I stay with my mommy and daddy?" Emma asked.

Emma and Lottie stared at Jay and Tim with anticipation. Tension blanketed the room as Jay struggled to think of a lie.

"Well...we have to make sure all three of you are healthy before we can let you live together," he lied.

"Alpha 411, I'm going to need you to come with me," Tim ordered.

"Just let me say bye to my baby," Lottie pleaded. Tim nodded and she rushed to hold Emma in a tight embrace. She kissed the top of her head before backing away. "Be good sweetheart. I'm going to see you again real soon."

"Okay mommy."

"I love you Ems."

"I love you too mommy." Emma didn't want to see her mother leave. She just wanted her family to be together and she didn't know it yet, but she wanted them to be free too.

Lottie blew her daughter a kiss as Jay and Tim escorted her out the room and ward. She knew she had to keep it together until she could go back into her cell and let it all out.

"So your daughter seemed nice," Tim pointed out in an attempt to ease the tension.

"She is," Lottie replied.

"How old is she?"

"Two."

"But I thought you've been in here for five years."

"I have."

"Then how can she be two?"

"You don't know a thing about this place, do you?"

"Not really."

"You'll learn."

Tim led Lottie into the same dreary interrogation room they were in before. They took their places at the table at the same time and stared each other down. Lottie knew Tim wanted to know more about the eternal flame but wasn't allowed to ask and she wasn't allowed to tell.

She made the decision to send her thoughts to his mind. *"I'll tell you all about this place but not in here."*

Tim gasped, caught completely off guard. He had never interrogated anyone like Lottie before and intended to find out how to get the necessary information out of her. But what he didn't know was that Lottie already had a plan for him.

"I heard you haven't said a word to anyone who works in this facility in years," Tim began. "Do you mind telling me the reason behind your decision?"

"When I first got here, I was willing to tell them everything they wanted to know. I thought I was helping my country," Lottie explained.

"Then what happened?"

"I realized what they're really up to in here."

"Which is what?"

"Your boss is about to barge in here."

"Tim, I'd appreciate it if you would accompany Alpha 411 to her room," Jay said as he rushed into the room.

"It's a prison cell," Lottie argued.

"Either way, you need to go back," Jay demanded.

"I know," Lottie snapped.

"Let's go," Tim urged. Lottie left the interrogation room and started back to her cell without acknowledging Tim's presence. Tim struggled to keep up so he grabbed Lottie's arm. "What happened in there?"

"What do you mean?"

"I heard your voice in my head."

"Keep your voice down," Lottie hissed.

"Tell me what happened."

"I can communicate telepathically and I know you have a lot of questions about this place. Your bosses are going to keep you in the dark and if they feel the need to provide an answer, odds are, it's going to be a lie."

"You can start by explaining how you have a two year old daughter when you've been in here five years."

"This place was built to keep psychics for experiments. One of those experiments is to see if a child with psychics for both parents will

21

become psychic. The Zulu Ward is where they keep the kids who were born here."

"What happens if a child born in here isn't psychic?"

Lottie didn't want to think about the answer but she knew telling Tim would work in her favor. "Execution."

"They kill innocent children?" Tim whispered, appalled by the new information.

"We're *all* innocent in here," Lottie began. "They kill anyone who isn't useful to them anymore."

Chapter 5

"I don't want to be here anymore," Sophie cried.

"None of us want to be here," Matt said.

"I can't be forced into these experiments and having kids. There has to be a way out of here."

"If there is, it won't be easy. Just stick with me and Lottie and you'll be fine until we can find a way out."

"Why did the guard call her Alpha 411?"

"They don't recognize names in here. When you get here, you're given a number and rank. Alphas are the elite psychics. They have multiple abilities and excel at all of them."

"They called me Alpha Bravo 911 when I got here, what does that mean?"

"An Alpha Bravo is someone who has multiple abilities, some they're really good at and others they're not," Matt explained.

"Were you always an Alpha?"

"No, I started out as a Bravo but with training, I moved up to Alpha Bravo and then Alpha."

"We get training in here?"

"Yes, and I suggest you take full advantage of it."

"Why?"

"If you want to survive this place, you need to develop as many abilities as possible and be really good at all of them," Matt began. "But you have to make sure to keep them from people you can't trust."

"How will I know who I can trust?"

"Lottie and I will help you."

"What are we helping with?" Lottie asked as she sat down next to Matt.

"We're going to tell Sophie who she can trust," Matt answered. "How's Emma?"

"She's nervous about being moved to the Zulu Yankee Ward but other than that she's fine."

"Are you alright?" Sophie asked. "You look upset."

"It always takes a lot out of me when I visit Emma," Lottie explained as she struggled to hold back tears.

"Alpha Bravo 911," a guard shouted.

"What do I do?" Sophie whispered in a panic.

"Look in his direction to find out what he wants," Matt answered.

As Sophie turned around the guard said, "Time for training."

"It'll be okay," Lottie reassured.

"Look for us when you get back," Matt added.

Sophie was terrified. She looked like she was heading towards her death. Matt and Lottie hoped she would make it out alive. As Sophie left with the guard, Lottie began to let her true emotions show.

"Don't you usually get taken back to your cell after you see Emma?" Matt asked.

"I convinced the new interrogator to bring me here."

"Why, what's wrong?"

"Why did you tell Emma to keep a secret?" Lottie angrily whispered. "We agreed not to put her through that until she could handle it."

"You saw her vision," Matt whispered. "What do you think they would have done with her if they found out!?"

"She's only two; she doesn't know how to shield certain thoughts from everyone."

Matt grabbed her hand. "Relax Lottie, I have it under control."

"I hope so Matt. It's bad enough she has to grow up as a prisoner with us but I couldn't handle it if we lost her."

"We won't lose her."

26

"You don't know that!"

"Yes I do, that vision was of the future, Lottie. It's going to happen eventually."

"You know just as well as I do that the future can easily change."

Matt put an arm around Lottie as she leaned her head against his shoulder. "It'll be okay."

As much as she didn't want to, Lottie finally let the tears flow down her face. "I hope so."

"What's the verdict on the new interrogator?"

"He's a good candidate. What about Sophie?"

"I think she might be the one," Matt answered excitedly.

Chapter 6

"Do you really kill people in here?" Tim asked angrily.

"I see you've been talking to Alpha 411," Jay replied.

"That wasn't an answer."

"I'm your boss, Tim. I don't have to answer you."

Tim wanted to argue and press for more information but refrained when he remembered Lottie's mention of executions. He thought he was important enough to make it out alive but didn't want to do anything to risk it. He had a family to think about.

"You know my reputation. Why bring me here?"

"We need you to make Alpha 411 talk."

"Why?"

"We need to know what she knows about an impending attack on the country," Jay replied.

"Why wouldn't she talk about that? Doesn't she realize how important this is?"

"She knows how heavily protected this facility is. She's not worried."

"She only has one weakness," Tim pointed out. "How do we use it to get her to talk?"

"Alpha 411 will do anything to keep her baby alive," Jay answered. "If we make her think Zulu 222 is going to die, she'll tell us anything we want to know."

"Don't you think that's cruel?"

"Not if it gets her to talk."

"Will it actually work?"

"I assume so."

"With something this important, we can't risk pushing her to the edge over a hunch. She could shut down completely or start a riot. I'm going to need to spend some time with her to make sure."

The perfectionist he was, Jay hated when his plans went off course even the tiniest bit. He wasn't allowed to tell Tim the truth about the facility. Even if he was allowed to tell him, he wouldn't. Jay loved knowing more than everyone else. He loved the power.

He attempted to regain his composure. "If you think it's necessary, you can take the time to talk to her. But the second you know how she will react to this plan, tell me."

"I will."

"Do whatever you have to just make it quick."

"You can't rush quality work."

"We don't have time for setbacks," Jay shouted.

"I will do my best to get her to talk as quickly as possible."

"I hope so."

Tim knew he was being lied to. His job was important to him and he didn't want to risk losing it. He was torn between doing his job and getting the answers he craved. But he was desperate for the truth and knew none of his bosses would tell him. There was only one person who would be willing to tell him everything he needed to know about the facility. Lottie.

Chapter 7

"Do you really think the interrogator will be willing to help us?" Matt asked worriedly.

"He'll do it. I know he will," Lottie began. "He's on his way to talk to me as we speak."

"How do you know he's not just going to rat us out?"

"Do you really need to question my skills?"

"You're the best at what you do but we both know how deceiving visions can be sometimes."

Lottie was offended by Matt's words. He knew her better than anyone else in the eternal flame. "Don't you think I can tell the difference!?"

"Lottie, I didn't mean it that way."

"I know Mattie," Lottie sighed. "I'm just so tired of being trapped in here and the new interrogator is our way out."

"We're all tired of being here."

Lottie sensed his energy, standing right behind her. "Timmy! I'm glad you're here." She turned to face him. "We have lots to talk about."

"How did you know I was here?" Tim asked with fear in his voice.

"It's what I do," Lottie answered.

Tim took a seat across from Matt and Lottie. "I talked to Jay."

"And I'm sure you know most of that conversation was a bunch of lies."

"He told me you have information about an impending attack on the country."

Matt laughed. "Is that what they're calling it now?"

"You mean that picture you showed me earlier."

"Yes."

"The man in that picture is Jay's dad. He has an inoperable brain tumor and Jay wants to

33

know if there's anything the healers can do to help him."

"He's been using you for his own selfish reasons?" Anger bubbled up within Tim. He didn't sign up for any of this. He didn't want any part in it. "Is that why you stopped cooperating?"

"After we had been here for a while, we realized what was really going on," Lottie explained. "People trying to find out information about their futures and then trying to learn how they could do all of this themselves."

"They could go to a local psychic for those things," Matt added. "They don't need to keep us trapped in here to get a reading."

"Which brings us to the real reason why we're all stuck in here," Lottie started.

"They want to turn us into weapons and become part of their psychic army," Matt finished.

"And that's why I refuse to cooperate. I have no interest in joining the army. If I did, I would have signed up already."

"They can't just keep you here against your will," Tim argued.

"The way they got us in here...they can," Lottie said. "This place is more than top secret, no one knows it exists unless they work or are imprisoned here."

"There has to be a way out," Tim offered.

"Many have tried and failed," Matt replied.

"Failed is an understatement," Lottie cut in.

Confusion danced across Tim's face. "What do you mean?"

"Anyone caught trying to escape gets killed," Lottie explained.

"How long are you supposed to stay here?" Matt asked.

"I don't know."

"Probably until he gets me to talk," Lottie pointed out.

Tim looked around nervously. "I didn't ask to be here."

Matt grabbed Lottie's hand. "Neither did we."

"Have you been able to see your family at all?" Lottie asked.

Tim shook his head. "No."

"I could show them to you...if you want," Lottie offered.

"How? We're trapped in here."

"It's a gift. One of my abilities is remote viewing."

"What's that?"

"It means she can see things from a distance," Matt explained.

Tears filled Tim's eyes. "I would love to see them."

"Look into my eyes," Lottie directed.

Tim did exactly as he was told and immediately saw his kids running around the living room. The twins seemed to have grown so much since he last saw them. He left them a month prior to his arrival at the facility so he could be read into everything he needed to know about the facility.

He watched his wife carry their six month old baby to the nursery and into her crib. She looked peaceful as she drifted off to sleep. He wished he could be there. His kids shouldn't have to grow up without him. Before he was ready, the image was taken away from him.

"Thank you," he whispered as he let tears pour down his cheeks. "Jay threatened them before I came here. It's good to know they're alright."

"I can keep checking on them to make sure nothing happens to them," Lottie offered.

"That would be great," Tim thanked. "I have to tell you something and I don't think you're going to like it."

"What is it?" Matt asked.

"Jay threatened your daughter."

"Emma," Lottie whispered.

"What did he say?" Matt asked suspiciously.

"He suggested making Lottie think your daughter is going to die in an attempt to get information."

Matt held onto Lottie tightly, knowing she couldn't handle the news. "Do you think it was an empty threat?"

"I doubt it."

"Jay doesn't make empty threats." Lottie tried to control her emotions but it was hard when it came to Emma. She was the only good thing to come from her forced captivity. It was the only thing that inspired Lottie to get up every morning for two years. "He's going to order Emma's execution tomorrow."

"That can't be true," Tim protested. "He said he would give me time before making the threat."

"He's already made up his mind," Lottie said through her sobs.

Tim struggled with the information. "We can't let him kill your daughter."

"We have to get Emma out of the Zulu Ward," Matt pointed out.

"Yeah, but how?" Tim asked.

Lottie's face lit up as something occurred to her. "I think I have an idea."

Chapter 8

"Hey Sophie," Matt greeted. "How was your first day of training?"

"It was great," Sophie answered with excitement. "I learned so much."

"Good," Lottie said.

"Who's this?" Sophie asked.

"That's Tim," Matt answered. "Tim, this is Sophie. She's new here too."

"You're not a prisoner here," Sophie pointed out.

"No," Tim replied. "I work here."

"You can trust him, Sophie," Lottie assured.

"He's going to help us," Matt added.

"How much can you tell me about this place?" Tim asked.

"Just about everything," Matt answered with a confidence Lottie admired.

"What do you want to know?" Lottie already knew the answer but didn't want to be rude. She found that it unnerved most people when they realized she could read their minds.

"How did you guys end up in here?"

"Matt and I were brought here on the same day," Lottie began. "We both fell for the same trick."

"What happened?" Sophie asked.

"The government already had psychics working for them when we got here," Matt explained. "They have ways of finding out who around the country is psychic."

"The day we were forced here, the government had their psychics issue a vision to everyone in the country. It was about a plot to assassinate the president."

"So you two must have felt the need to warn him about it," Tim assumed.

"Us and hundreds of others," Lottie replied.

"At first we thought they were bringing us in to give every detail about our vision," Matt started. "But when we were thrown into prison cells, we realized what was really going on."

Lottie decided to answer Tim's question before he could ask. "There was never going to be an assassination attempt on the president. It was just a trick to trap us in here."

"How did you two meet?" Sophie asked.

"I first saw her on the drive in. Once we got here everyone was lined up and given a number, we were placed next to each other," Matt explained.

"He's Alpha 410 and I'm Alpha 411," Lottie added. "Matt saw how scared I was during the lineup and tried to comfort me. We've pretty much been inseparable since."

"What about you Sophie?" Tim asked. "How did you end up in here?"

Sophie was hesitant to answer. Her story wasn't as tame as the one Matt and Lottie told. She didn't want them to think she was a bad person.

"It's okay," Lottie softly said. She already knew the whole story and didn't think any differently of her.

Sophie took a deep breath as if it would be her last. "I was in school and fell asleep during class. I had a dream that I was in a burning building and when I woke up, the classroom was on fire."

"It wasn't your fault," Matt reassured.

"No one knew what started the fire except me," Sophie began. "I felt terrible about what I did so I tried to put out the fire. When I made a ball of water in my hand, one of my classmates saw and told the police about it. The police came to me asking questions I couldn't answer and they said I had to be taken to the station for more questioning but instead of a police station, I ended up in here."

"It was a friend who turned you in, wasn't it?" Lottie asked.

Sophie nodded. "She was the only one I could talk to about what I had been going through." Tears welled in her eyes. "And she betrayed me."

"It's okay Sophie," Matt said. "We're going to get out of here."

"How do you know we'll make it out alive?" she asked.

"I saw my daughter's vision," Lottie answered. "She saw us living in a house away from this place."

"Do you have any suggestions for how we can get out of here?" Tim asked.

"First we'll have to get Emma out of the Zulu Ward. I have a plan for that."

Chapter 9

Matt was back in his cell waiting for Lottie to reveal her big plan. He wondered why she left so abruptly before telling anyone about it. But he knew Lottie well enough to know not to distract her when she was on a mission. He turned his head at the sound of his cell door squeak open.

"Lottie, how did you get in here?"

"I have my ways."

"Are you going to tell me about this plan of yours?"

"Oh Mattie, don't you know better by now?"

Confusion spread across Matt's face. "What do you mean?"

"You know, I never did like how act so...what's the word I'm looking for? Dumb."

Matt knew Lottie wasn't acting like herself. "Why are you acting this way?"

"Don't you know?"

"Alright, that's enough Liam."

Matt turned around to see Lottie standing outside his cell smiling at him. He turned back to see the Lottie who was in his cell morph into a familiar face. "Does someone want to fill me in?"

"Matt, you remember Liam," Lottie began.

"Yeah," Matt answered. "He was my cellmate when we first got here."

"I discovered I have the ability to change my appearance to whatever I want," Liam explained. "Lottie told me you need help breaking your daughter out of the Zulu Ward."

"So you'll help us?"

"Of course, that's why Lottie had me do this. She wanted you to see me in action."

Matt turned to face Lottie. "What's the plan?"

"The three of us are going to go to Emma's room and Liam, pretending to be Jay is going to tell the guards he needs to take Emma for testing."

"Where are we going to keep Emma until we can get out of this place?" Matt asked.

"I haven't figured it out yet," Lottie answered. "We can't just keep her in our cells, someone will notice."

"It won't be long before someone realizes she's missing from the Zulu Ward," Liam pointed out.

"We'll have to escape right after we get Emma back," Matt added.

"How?" Lottie asked. "We haven't had enough time to come up with a plan."

There was a twinkle in Liam's eyes as he thought of a plan. "What if I pretend to be Jay again to get you guys out?"

"That's dangerous," Matt said.

"If you get caught, you could be killed," Lottie added.

"It's a risk I'm willing to take," Liam declared. "If I can get you guys out you can at least be safe and figure out a way to shut this place down."

"We would have to act fast," Matt pointed out. "Who knows what they'll do when they realize we're missing."

"Liam, I think you should just take Matt and Emma out of here," Lottie suggested. "If I'm gone, the tyrants here will notice right away."

"No, Lottie, I'm not leaving you behind," Matt protested.

"Excuse me, Lottie," Tim said nervously as he entered the prison cell. "You're wanted back in the interrogation room."

Lottie nodded at Tim and then turned to face Matt. "We'll talk more about this later." She walked past everyone to exit the cell. "So Timmy, why am I being summoned this time?"

"I don't know, Jay only told me to bring you in."

"That can't be good."

"Why not? What do you think is going to happen?"

"I don't know," Lottie began. "Someone's blocking Jay's thoughts from me. That's the problem."

"Is there anything you can do?"

"Not until I find out who's helping Jay."

"How can I help?"

"I don't think it's going to be hard to find out, Jay's definitely going to want to gloat."

To say Tim was worried was an understatement. His stomach was in knots. He just wanted to be with his family again. "What does this mean for our escape plan?"

"I don't think it's a good idea to talk about that right now." Lottie wasn't sure if it was because she could feel Tim's emotions but her stomach was in knots too. She knew something bad was going to be revealed to her once she entered the interrogation room.

Tim opened the door and for the first time in five years, Lottie was hesitant to go in.

For the first time she didn't know what to expect. She knew she couldn't let anyone see how nervous she was so she created a white protective shield around her body and walked through the door.

Lottie sat down in her usual seat and waited for Jay to enter with his helper. She looked at Tim wanting to ask what was going to happen but she didn't want anyone else to know what they were up to.

"Jay should be in soon," Tim said uncomfortably as he took his place across from Lottie.

It wasn't long before Jay entered the room with his secret weapon close behind. Lottie wasn't prepared for what she saw. She couldn't let Jay see how much the revelation had impacted her. She had to pretend she didn't care even though she did.

Jay had a mischievous smile on his face. He knew he had something special. "Alpha 411, I believe you've met my new colleague Alpha Bravo 911."

"Sophie," Lottie began. "I have to admit I didn't see this coming."

"Lottie, I didn't want…" Sophie trailed off. She knew Lottie didn't want to hear her excuses.

"I've seen inside your head Sophie," Lottie said telepathically. *"I know you wouldn't have done this without good reason. You're going to explain everything to me."*

"Unlike you, Alpha Bravo 911 is willing to help me," Jay gloated. "She told me about my father."

"Then you know there's nothing anyone can do," Lottie replied.

"I refuse to believe that!" Jay yelled. "There has to be a way to help him."

"If you get a healer to work on him, he will die," Lottie explained.

Jay appeared tortured by Lottie's words. "How could a healer kill him?"

"I can't tell you."

Jay looked desperately at Sophie. "Please...tell me."

Sophie looked apprehensively at Lottie. Lottie stared back not giving any indication of what she should do. "Some people are marked for death and it doesn't matter what anyone does to try to keep them alive, they will die when they're supposed to."

"What do you mean marked for death?" Jay asked.

"Everyone dies at some point," Sophie explained. "When someone is marked for death it means they're going to die soon."

"What do you mean by soon? How much longer does my father have to live?"

Sophie looked back at Lottie for guidance. But Lottie didn't give her any help. She just sat there expressionless. Sophie felt a little hurt by Lottie's unwillingness to help. She promised to help and when Sophie needed it, Lottie wasn't doing a thing.

"He has one month left," she answered weakly.

"Traitor," Lottie mumbled.

"Excuse me?" Sophie asked timidly. She knew Lottie was much more powerful than her and didn't want to get into a fight.

"It's okay," Lottie answered telepathically. *"I know the truth. We need to get out of here right away."*

"Girls," Tim warned.

"I said you're a traitor," Lottie stated loudly.

"I'm doing what I can to survive!" Sophie yelled.

"You won't survive this place if you betray everyone who's trapped here!"

"Enough!" Jay shouted. "Both of you get out."

Without saying a word Sophie and Lottie left the interrogation room. They walked in awkward silence towards the cafeteria. Sophie wanted to explain herself but wasn't sure how Lottie would react. Lottie already knew everything she needed to know and had already come up with a plan.

Chapter 10

"What's wrong?" Matt asked as Lottie and Sophie approached the table.

"You told Sophie to help Jay," Lottie accused.

"Let me explain," he pleaded.

"No need, I already know everything."

"Then what's the problem?"

Lottie struggled to keep herself calm. "Why didn't you tell me about this first?"

"We were short on time and I couldn't find you."

"I was working on a plan to keep our daughter safe," Lottie yelled.

"I know that now," Matt shouted.

"What's going to happen to me?" Sophie asked.

"You're going to be fine," Matt assured. "We're going to use this to our advantage."

"Jay threatened your life," Lottie began. "And the truth is he can't kill you unless you're proven to be useless. Trust me, that won't happen."

"So what's the plan?" Sophie asked.

"We need to use him to get us out of here," Matt pointed out.

"Even if we manage to get out of here, this place will still exist and there are plenty more people locked up," Lottie started. "We have to find a way to get everyone out of here and shut this place down."

"How?" Matt asked. "I think the guards will notice if everyone's gone."

"That's not our only problem," Sophie stated. "We have no clue how to get out of here."

"There's a plan in the works to get us out but to get everyone else out of here is going to require a lot more work," Lottie replied.

"Before we leave we're going to have to make sure everyone else knows how to escape," Matt suggested.

"Are you suggesting what I think you are?" Sophie asked hesitantly.

"We're going to escape," Lottie whispered.

Matt felt his stomach drop. "But no one has ever pulled it off."

"Then let's be the first to do it," Lottie said confidently.

"What's the plan?" Sophie asked.

"We have to get Emma out of the Zulu Ward," Lottie answered.

Matt anxiously scratched the back of his head. "Where would we hide her?"

"We'll figure something out," Lottie started. "Maybe Liam can help with that. All I know is I'm not leaving my baby where she's in danger."

"Once we get your daughter, how are we going to figure out how to get everyone else out?" Sophie asked.

"And what about the rest of the Zulu Ward?" Matt asked.

"Every parent will want to get their kids out before they escape," Lottie answered. "We'll have Liam and other shifters help them get the kids out."

"What about the orphans?" Matt pointed out.

Lottie's heart ached as she thought about all of the children in the Zulu Ward whose parents were executed. "First we'll have to figure out how many of them there are and then have the shifters help us get them out."

Matt got up from the table. "Let's get to it."

Chapter 11

"Are you sure this is a good idea?" Sophie asked hesitantly.

"It's the only plan we have," Lottie answered.

"If you're too scared you can go back," Liam suggested.

Lottie glared at Liam. "Be nice."

"We shouldn't be here," Sophie whispered.

"I'm allowed," Matt said. "I have a daughter in here."

"She's my daughter too," Lottie snapped.

Matt stopped and grabbed Lottie's hand. "I know. My point was that we're allowed in here."

"Only with supervision," Lottie pointed out.

"That's what I'm here for," Liam said proudly.

"I told you not to talk, you don't sound a thing like Jay," Lottie snapped.

They walked down until they came to Emma's room. Lottie nervously opened the door, knowing that once her plan was set into motion, they had to act quickly. She stood in the doorway for a moment, watching her daughter sleep peacefully. She wanted her daughter to grow up with that same peace rather than the fear and misery of being held prisoner.

"Mommy?" Emma sleepily asked. "Why are you here so late?"

Lottie picked Emma up and carried her out the door. "You get to live with me and Daddy now."

"Really?" she yawned.

"Yes," Matt answered as he kissed the top of Emma's head. "We can be a family now."

"We have to get her out of here before someone sees us," Liam said. "Where are we taking her?"

"I'm not letting her out of my sight," Lottie replied. "We'll take her back to my cell."

"I'm staying with you," Matt added.

Lottie shifted Emma in her arms. "That's fine."

Once they reached Lottie's cell, she put Emma down on her bed. She sat by her side and watched her sleep. "Bring Tim over here."

"Are you sure that's a good idea?" Matt asked. "We don't know how he'll react to all of this."

"He's going to help us. I know he will."

Matt trusted Lottie's judgment. He left to find Tim but didn't need to look very long. "Tim, I was just looking for you."

"I think I know why. Where's Lottie?" Tim asked.

Matt led Tim to Lottie's cell but something felt wrong. He stopped at the door, hoping Lottie would figure out what was going on. From inside the cell, Lottie realized what was happening. She learned about Tim's intentions and thought of a way to get out of the situation.

"Matt, wait for me inside," Lottie said as she stepped outside while barely opening the door. Lottie watched as Matt went inside to look after Emma, being careful not to open the door too wide. "I think we have a problem here, Timmy."

"What do you mean?" Tim asked nervously.

"I'm not dumb. I can see your thoughts and every intention. I know you're the best interrogator in the country and I also know that you've been putting on an act to try to gain my trust in the hopes I would open up to you."

"How long have you known?"

"Since I first met you."

"Are you sure about that?" he asked suspiciously. "You seemed to trust me for a moment there."

"You're not the only one who knows how to get what you want, Timmy."

"What's that supposed to mean?"

"You're smart, you'll figure it out."

"Cut the crap, I know you kidnapped your daughter. What I don't know is how you pulled it off."

Lottie stood there in silence. She knew Tim didn't have to be psychic to know when she was lying. She could still use him to escape whether he wanted to or not. As much as she wanted to stop talking to him altogether, she knew that in order for her plan to work, she would have to stay friendly.

"What do you think you know?" Lottie asked.

"Come with me," Tim insisted.

"I'm not going back to the interrogation room."

"You don't have any other choice."

"Are you sure about that Timmy? Because I happen to know a bit of information about your family that would interest you. You should actually be worried."

Tim's eyes widened in fear. "Who have you told?"

"Not a soul," Lottie replied innocently. "But if I were you I would worry more about someone around here finding out than anything I may or may not have planned."

"How do I know you're not lying just to get your way?"

Lottie stepped closer to Tim and whispered. "Your wife is trying to find you. It's only a matter of time before she brings your psychic child here."

Tim gasped, shocked that Lottie really knew his situation. "What do you want me to do?"

"Get me and my family out of here without drawing attention to us."

"And what's in it for me?"

"I'll protect your family from the people here."

"You can't guarantee their safety."

Lottie laughed. "You obviously don't know me very well. They'll be safe with me, I promise."

After a moment of thought, Tim finally spoke. "How do I get you all out of here?"

Chapter 12

"Are you sure this is going to work?" Tim asked reluctantly.

"It'll get us out of here," Lottie answered. "But they'll notice we're gone pretty quickly."

"You won't be able to go back there," Matt added. "It won't be long before they realize that you're the one who got us out."

"And if they catch you," Lottie began. "You're as good as dead."

"After they interrogate you, of course."

"You and your family will have to stay with us until all of this is over."

"I can't just uproot them like that," Tim protested.

Lottie moved closer to Tim, hoping no one would hear her. "If you don't, they'll kill your family too. It doesn't matter if they're children, anyone who gets in their way dies."

"They wouldn't really do that, would they?" Tim asked with worry in his voice.

Matt put an arm around Lottie as he spoke. "They kill some of the babies who were born in this place; they won't hesitate to kill children on the outside."

Sadness spread across Tim's face. "They killed one of your kids, didn't they?"

Lottie couldn't bear to look Tim in the eye. It was the first time in years she had shown real weakness to anyone other than Matt. "They killed more than one of them. Emma is our only living child."

Liam rushed into Lottie's cell. "They're coming. If you ever hope to make it out alive, you have to leave now."

"Does Sophie know the plan?" Matt asked.

"We both do," Liam answered.

"Take care of her. If anything happens to her, I'll find out about it."

"I know, Lottie, now leave!"

Tim casually walked away, trying not to raise suspicion. Lottie held onto Emma tightly as she followed closely behind him. Matt walked next to Lottie, looking around to be sure they weren't followed.

Tim stopped at an office door. "Wait here."

Lottie watched nervously as he entered the office. She could feel her stomach twisting as they waited for Tim to return. She had never attempted an escape before and the thought of what would happen if they were caught was terrifying to her. Every second felt like an eternity.

Matt leaned in towards Lottie and spoke softly. "Hey, it'll be okay. We're going to get out of here."

Tim left the office carrying a duffel bag. "Ready?"

Matt and Lottie nodded as they watched Emma sleep in Lottie's arms. They made their way towards a room they hadn't seen since their arrival five years ago. Memories flooded Lottie's head as she saw all of the military vehicles parked inside.

She remembered sitting in the back of one of those vehicles, terrified of what was going to happen when they finally stopped. That was when she saw Matt for the first time. He gave her a reassuring smile, as if to wordlessly say that everything was going to be alright. Bringing her back to the present moment, Lottie felt Matt squeeze her hand.

"Get in the back and change out of those prison uniforms. I'll drive us away from here," Tim said as he handed Matt a pile of clothes.

Lottie gave Emma to Matt as her stomach churned while she climbed into the back of the vehicle. She leaned down to get Emma back so Matt could climb in after. Her anxiety really kicked in when she heard the door slam shut. She sat down and tried to calm herself down.

"It's okay Lottie, we're getting out of here," Matt whispered.

"I didn't think it would affect me this much," Lottie began. "Remembering being brought here just as we're trying to escape from this place…"

"I know."

"Do you think Tim will be able to get us out of here without any problems?"

"I can hear you guys back there!" Tim shouted from the driver's seat as he started driving away. "You might want to be quiet until we're out of here."

"Let us know when it's safe," Matt called.

Once they changed into regular clothes, they sat back down and Lottie rested her head on Matt's shoulder, trying to keep it together. Matt held onto Lottie, hoping it would bring her some comfort. They could feel each bump in the road as they continued forward. After what seemed like an eternity, they were slowing down.

"We're near the front gate," Lottie whispered.

When they came to a stop, Lottie and Matt could hear Tim speaking with the guard at the gate. Lottie wanted so badly to get inside the guard's head so they could leave faster but she knew it was too risky. Using her remote viewing, Lottie nervously watched the scene unfold.

"Aren't you the new interrogator?" The guard asked. "What are you doing driving this vehicle off the property?"

"I was ordered to go pick up some new recruits," Tim answered.

"Do you have your paperwork?"

"I do," Tim replied as he reached for the papers on the dashboard.

Everyone's stomach flipped as they nervously waited for the guard's approval. He lifted his radio to his face and spoke, "open up."

Matt and Lottie breathed a sigh of relief as they heard the gate open and Tim drove off. They were finally out but had to quickly get a new car. It wasn't long before they came to a stop and Tim let them out. They were on a road in the middle of nowhere.

"I'm taking this vehicle where it's supposed to go, you two find a car and meet me at my house."

"But Tim," Matt protested. "We don't know where we are or how to drive."

"Matt, we can't go with him, it's too dangerous."

"Then what are we supposed to do?"

"We'll figure it out."

Matt didn't seem too sure about this plan but he knew there was no other way. He knew the important thing was keeping Emma safe.

"Take my phone," Tim said as he threw his phone towards Matt. "I'll call you when I get home and pick you up."

Lottie shook her head. "I don't think that's a good idea."

"Why not?" Matt asked.

"Once they realize we're all missing they'll track your phone."

"Lottie, they have some of the most powerful psychics working for them. Forget about tracking the phone, they'll track us instead!"

"There has to be a way we can stay hidden from them," Tim said.

"I can keep us hidden," Lottie replied. "That doesn't help us stay in touch."

"We'll have to keep the phone on until we get back together," Matt suggested. "Let's just hope no one's looking for us before then."

"I better go now," Tim insisted. "The faster we get back together, the better."

"Be safe," Lottie said.

"Hopefully we'll see you soon," Matt added.

They watched reluctantly as Tim drove away. Lottie held her daughter tight in an attempt to comfort herself.

Chapter 13

"Where do we go now?" Matt asked.

"We have to find the closest town."

"What then?"

"Then we'll lay low until Tim can come get us."

"Is it really a good idea to stay in one spot for a while?"

"Probably not," Lottie answered. "Everything depends on Emma. If she needs to eat or use the bathroom, we'll have to stop."

"You're right, otherwise, we keep moving."

"Agreed."

They walked on the side of the road, hoping no one would bother them along the way. Emma was sound asleep in Lottie's arms and she hoped it would stay that way, at least for a while. Matt was struggling to hide his worry. They escaped from the eternal flame but he knew things were far from over. He knew it wouldn't be long before the manhunt began.

"Are you alright?" Lottie asked with concern in her voice.

"I don't know," Matt sighed. "I just have a bad feeling about all of this."

"We both knew doing this was going to make our lives ten times harder."

"You're right Lottie, but do we really want our daughter to grow up in this life?"

"This is better than her being a prisoner for the rest of her life...besides, this is temporary. We won't always be running from the eternal flame."

"This is the first time we've been outside in years," Matt began. "I want to enjoy it but I'm so afraid of it all being taken away from us."

"That's an even better reason to enjoy as much as we can while we're still able to."

For the first time in years, they enjoyed the crisp fresh air, the breeze gently blowing the sweet scent of flowers to their noses. They nearly forgot what it was like to feel the warm rays of the sun on their skin. Excitement filled the pair as they saw the first signs of civilization.

"Where do you think we are?"

"I don't know," Lottie answered. "I think it would be suspicious for us to ask around."

"Right, we really don't want to attract any sort of attention to us."

Emma yawned as she woke up. A look of awe spread across her face as she saw the outside world for the first time in her life. "Mommy where are we?"

Lottie looked at Matt, unsure of what to say. She wasn't entirely sure of where exactly they were. "We're finding a new home."

"Where are we going to live?" Emma asked.

"We're not sure yet," Matt replied.

"Are you hungry, Emma?"

"A little," she answered.

"We'll find somewhere to eat."

"Tim didn't leave us much money so we'll have to make it last."

"I'll be fine until Tim comes to get us, he shouldn't be too long."

"Lottie, you know I can't let you do that."

Lottie smiled. "You're always trying to take care of me."

He laughed. "Someone has to."

"Let's find someplace to eat."

They came across a diner and walked inside, eager to taste real food again. When they reached the table they gulped down their water. They were kept underfed and dehydrated in the eternal flame. They ate until their stomachs were full, something that hadn't happened in years. The phone Tim gave them rang as they left the diner.

"Hello?"

"Matt, where are you guys? I can come pick you up now."

"I'm not exactly sure. We walked into the town closest to where you dropped us off. We just left a diner."

"I know exactly where that is, stay put. I'll be there in fifteen minutes."

Without a goodbye, Tim hung up.

"What did he say?" Lottie asked. "Is he coming to get us now?"

"He'll be here in fifteen minutes."

"That seems like a long time to stay in one place."

"It is but it's the only way he'll find us." Matt realized how worried Lottie was and grabbed her hand. "We'll be alright. Tim will be here soon."

"I just don't like being out in the open like this. Someone could be looking for us and we're making it easy for them to get to us."

"I know."

It was the longest fifteen minutes they'd ever experienced. Emma didn't fully understand what was going on but even she felt scared. The family sat on a bench holding tightly to each other in an attempt for comfort. Lottie could barely focus on anything.

"Matt, Lottie, get in."

"Thank God," Lottie whispered.

They climbed in the van as quickly as possible, finally able to breathe. Tim sped off as soon as the doors were closed, not even giving them a chance to buckle in.

"I have to pick up my family," Tim said. "We're going to need a bigger van."

"Do you have access to a bigger van?" Matt asked.

"I do but they'll be able to track it."

"Then we can't use it," Lottie panicked.

It was like a light bulb went off in Tim's head. "Maybe we can."

"How?" Matt and Lottie asked at the same time.

"I have a cabin in the mountains. No one knows about it. We can drive to one location so they track us there and hike up to the cabin."

"Is that such a good idea? We have kids to think about," Lottie replied.

"It's not too bad of a hike; my kids do it all the time."

"Alright," Matt agreed. "Let's try to get there as fast as possible."

Chapter 14

"How are we supposed to do this without Matt and Lottie?" Sophie asked in a panicked tone.

"We have no other choice, they're gone now and it's up to us to act out their plan," Liam replied.

"I'm new here. No one is going to listen to me."

Liam put a hand on Sophie's shoulder in an attempt to comfort her. He wasn't used to comforting people but he needed her to stay calm. "Lottie trusts you with this, as soon as they hear that, they'll listen to whatever you have to say."

"Why didn't she put you in charge of this?"

"Because she knows me too well, she knows I won't be able to convince them."

"She doesn't trust you?"

"Not fully."

"Why not?" Sophie asked.

"Matt, Lottie and I were all brought here on the same day. A week after that, they started recruiting for their army." Liam didn't want to tell the rest of the story. "I was the only one who broke."

"What does that mean?"

"They managed to convince me that joining their army was a good idea. Lottie hated me for it."

"If you joined their army, why are you here?"

Liam shook his head as tears formed in the corner of his eye. He needed to appear strong. "I didn't know what I had signed up for. The day I joined, I abandoned the army. I tried running away but didn't get very far before I was caught."

Sophie was fully absorbed in the story. She could see and feel every detail of the event as Liam spoke. "What happened next?"

"The man in charge of the unit I was in took me to be executed. I was moments away from death when they discovered I have a highly valuable ability. I was so scared that I didn't even know I was shape-shifting."

"So they brought you back here?"

"Yeah, they wanted me to learn how to control it before they could use me again."

"What did Lottie do when she found out you were back?"

"Like I said before, she hated me for what I did," Liam began. "We became pretty good friends in that first week. She doesn't take betrayals lightly."

"She was furious," Sophie said, suddenly able to see exactly what happened. "She yelled at you about how she couldn't trust you anymore."

"And I've spent years trying to make up for what I did."

"Lottie didn't seem to be angry with you when she was here."

"Things have gotten a lot better between us over the years but she still doesn't fully trust me."

"What did Matt think about all of this?"

"He was more forgiving. We all went through the same thing when they were trying to recruit us. Matt knew how awful it was and never held it against me."

Liam's story scared Sophie. She didn't want to endure all the pain her new friends had already been through. "I guess we should get started now."

"How are you feeling? You look nervous."

"That's exactly how I feel. It's a lot of pressure on me."

"Start with the other new guys who you came here with. People who were brought here together tend to find a bond."

Sophie nodded and walked over to the table where a group of young psychics were sitting. They were all new and scared. But they welcomed Sophie when she asked to sit with them. She was just as scared, not only because she was new in the eternal flame but because she knew failing Lottie wasn't an option.

"Do you really think that's possible?" a girl the same age as Sophie asked.

"I know it is," Sophie replied. "My friends I told you about, Matt and Lottie, they got out of here with their daughter. They're free."

"Isn't someone around here going to notice they're gone?" A boy asked.

"Eventually they will if they haven't already," Sophie answered. "I'm waiting for a signal from Lottie. She's going to let me know when to start. Can I count on you guys?"

Everyone at the table nodded.

Sophie went around the rest of the facility talking to everyone she could. It wasn't long before the plan had reached all of the prisoners inside the eternal flame. They were all on board and for the first time since the facility had taken its first prisoner, the air was filled with hope.

"You did it Sophie," Liam said as he patted her back. "Lottie would be proud."

"I know," she sighed. "Things are just going to get harder now."

"Yeah but it'll be worth it in the end."

"I don't know if I'm ready for what comes next."

Chapter 15

"Mommy my feet hurt," Emma whined. "Are we there yet?"

"Almost, sweetheart," Lottie answered.

Lottie, Matt and Emma were obviously exhausted while Tim and his family didn't seem to be the least bit tired. That was the difference between freedom and being held prisoner for years.

"We should be there in a few minutes," Tim said.

Despite being exhausted, Lottie knew she needed to focus enough to ensure their safety. "Matt you should make sure no one's following us while I make sure there's no one waiting for us at the cabin."

Matt went to the back of the group and scanned the tree line for any sign of other people. "We're good on my end."

"Same," Lottie added. "We're the only ones up here. Let's get inside."

A sense of relief washed over Matt and Lottie as they finally entered the cabin. Sore and worn-out from the hike, Matt, Emma and Lottie all immediately threw themselves on the couch. It didn't take Emma long to fall asleep. Lottie held onto her sleeping daughter, struggling to keep herself awake.

"It's okay," Matt whispered. "You should get some sleep too."

"I don't want to. What if something happens?"

"Lottie you look beat, you need to get some rest. I'll wake you up if we need you for anything."

She yawned. "Promise?"

Matt kissed Emma and Lottie on their foreheads. "I promise."

It was all Lottie needed to hear to finally allow herself to close her eyes.

Matt watched them sleep for a moment before turning to Tim. "There's no way anyone can find us up here, right?"

"There aren't any trails leading up here," Tim replied. "I built this place to make sure I could be alone with my family without anyone coming to bother us."

"I just have to be sure. You understand?"

"Of course."

"Is anyone going to tell me what's going on?" Tim's wife, Mary asked.

Matt glanced in Tim's direction uncomfortably. He didn't want to be the one to explain the situation. It was bad enough to live through it.

Tim took a deep breath as he decided whether or not to tell the truth. "That place was horrible, Mary. You have no idea. I had to escape."

"Escape?" she asked. "Does that mean you're in trouble?"

"We all are," Tim answered.

Fear spread across Mary's face. "What did you guys do?"

"Mary," Matt interrupted. "What Tim means to say is that we're all in danger. The place we escaped from will be looking for all of us if they aren't already."

"So you're saying that me and my children are also in danger?"

"I'm so sorry Mary," Tim pleaded. "That's why I brought us all here."

Mary's face became expressionless as she struggled to process the new information. It seemed as though all time had stopped for a moment. No one was entirely sure of what to expect from her. Matt found himself wondering if she was going to be a problem. He had his own family to think about and wouldn't hesitate to leave Tim and his family behind if it meant saving Emma and Lottie.

"Matt?" Lottie sleepily asked. "Is everything okay?"

Matt took her hand. "Everything is fine."

Matt's lie snapped Lottie awake. She sat up and stared into Matt's eyes. "What is it?"

Matt sent his concerns to Lottie's head. *"We may need to leave. I think Mary's going to be a problem for us."*

"Why?"

"She didn't seem too happy to hear that her family is in danger."

"No sane person would be happy with that, Matt. Give her a chance."

Lottie knew Matt well enough to know that his instincts were always right. But she needed to see for herself what was going through Mary's mind before agreeing to Matt's plan. She turned her focus towards Mary and looked inside her mind.

Mary still hadn't spoken a word since she realized her family was in danger. Lottie saw just how many different thoughts were swirling around her mind. When she saw that Mary was seriously considering calling the police for help, Lottie knew she had to get her family as far away as possible.

"Please tell me you have a plan, Matt."

"I'm working on it."

"We have to get out of here as soon as we can."

"What about Tim?"

"Are you two alright?" Tim asked. "You guys look like something's bothering you."

"We're alright," Lottie answered.

"Just fine," Matt said at the same time.

"What are we going to do now?"

Matt and Lottie glanced at each other, unsure of what to tell Tim. They had every intensions of leaving him and his family behind. There was no way either of them were going to tell the truth.

"If we really are safe up here then there's nothing we need to do right now," Lottie replied.

Mary suddenly snapped out of her stupor. "You mean we're just going to sit here and wait for the danger to come? I'm not just going to sit here and let my family get hurt. We should call the police, let them do their jobs and protect us. Anything but sit here with targets on our backs!"

Matt felt like he couldn't breathe as he tried to keep himself calm. "The police won't be able to help us."

"How do you know?"

"Because we're dealing with a secret government facility that has access to their own army," Lottie answered. "The police have no authority over them."

"Timmy, what did you get us into?"

"I didn't know what I was getting myself into when I accepted the job," Tim replied apologetically.

"There's no use in fighting about this now," Lottie interrupted. "What's done is done."

"You guys are parents too. Don't you want to protect your daughter?"

"Of course we do," Matt said. "But you don't know what we're dealing with. Lottie and

I were held prisoner there for five years; we have a pretty good idea of what's coming."

"I'm sorry, I have to do what's best for my family," Mary cried.

Lottie panicked and blurted out what she knew would only make the situation worse. "If you involve the police, you're only killing you and your entire family. Everyone who ever knew you will be dead and it'll be entirely *your* fault!"

The cabin fell silent. Lottie stared at the ground, feeling the stares of everyone judging her for her harsh words. Matt knew she was right but that she should have found a better way of getting her point across.

"Maybe we should leave," Matt calmly suggested.

"You can't leave," Tim argued. "You have nowhere to go."

"I think we've done enough damage. We'll figure something out."

"Matt, you have a daughter to think about. You can't just take her away from an environment like this."

"That's not up to you Tim," Lottie interrupted. "If Matt and I want to take her someplace else then that's our decision."

"But where will you go?"

"It's probably for the best if you don't know."

Matt put a hand on Lottie's shoulder. "Are you sure about this, Lottie? Maybe we should stay here until we can find somewhere else to go."

Without saying a word, Lottie put her hands on Matt's face and showed him what was in their future. The cabin was surrounded by soldiers, both psychic and not. Guns mixed with psychic abilities meant they didn't stand a chance. They were outnumbered and outgunned. In the end, every single one of them was dead.

"We can't let this happen, Lottie."

"That's why we have to leave."

"We can't just leave Tim and his family behind, they'll all die."

"Mary is a threat to us, Matt. We can't stay with her."

"We have to at least give them a chance. They don't deserve to die."

Lottie sighed. "We all have to get out of here right away."

"What? Why?" Tim asked in confusion.

"I'll tell you later, right now we need to leave!"

Chapter 16

"Are you sure that's what Lottie said?" Liam asked. "It doesn't sound like something she would do."

"Something must have happened," Sophie answered. "Why else would she be on the move again so soon?"

Liam leaned in close and whispered so no one else could hear him. "No one in here seems to know they're gone. How could her vision happen?"

"Maybe they do know but they're not letting it show to the rest of us."

"No, someone would have picked up a thought about all of this. They're clueless here."

"I don't know about that. Something doesn't feel right."

"What is it?"

"What if the psychic soldiers are hiding people's thoughts around here?"

Liam's stomach knotted. "If that's the case, then Matt and Lottie are in more trouble than we thought."

Sophie gasped. "What can we do to help them?"

"There's not much we can do from in here."

"We can't just sit here and let them die. They don't deserve that."

"None of us deserve this, Sophie. But we're trapped here while they're out there. All we can do is send Matt and Lottie as much information as we can."

"And since the people here are being helped by their army, we can't tell them what they're planning."

"We might have to come up with a new plan."

Sophie and Liam sat there in silence, trying to come up with another way to help their friends. Many thoughts raced through their minds, most of which they dismissed right away. They knew they had to wait for the perfect moment to start the riots. They knew the chance of them dying was high but it was a risk they were willing to take.

"I hate to say this," Liam began. "But I think we need to start the riots early."

"Are you crazy!?" Sophie whispered.

"Matt and Lottie need every ounce of help they can get. The riots will distract the army enough to keep them away."

Sophie shook her head. "I don't like this."

"I know you're scared, we all are. But we have to do this...for them."

"How are we going to shut this place down if the riots happen too soon?"

"We can't worry about that right now."

"Liam, the whole point of Lottie's plan is to make sure this place closes for good."

"Then we'll start another riot when the time is right. We need to do this now."

"There might not be enough of us left by then. We can't take that risk. We have to trust that Matt and Lottie can handle themselves."

"Lottie wouldn't have told you about her change of plan if she didn't need help," Liam argued. "I know her better than you do."

Sophie rubbed her forehead where she felt a headache forming. "I think we should wait to hear from Lottie again. Let her clarify things for us."

"You do what you want, Sophie, I'm going to get this thing started."

Liam left Sophie alone at the table as he went to talk to everyone willing to listen. Only the people who were there long enough to know Matt and Lottie agreed to help. It was exactly what Liam expected.

Sophie couldn't catch her breath. Terror filled her as the thought of failure and even worse, death crossed her mind. *"Lottie if you can hear me, we need to talk right now."*

Lottie's voice sounded concerned in Sophie's head. *"Sophie, what's wrong?"*

"It's Liam, he's trying to start the riot early. He says you need the help right now."

"No, we're on our way to a new safe house. Tell him not to do anything."

"I'll let him know. But Lottie, there's something else…"

"What is it?"

"We think psychic soldiers are helping the people working here. We can't read anyone's thoughts."

"That's not good. They must know we're gone."

"But no one is letting on that they know. What does this mean?"

"It means they're planning something horrible." Lottie paused for a moment. "Maybe you should let Liam continue with his plan. It'll catch them off guard and we might be able to get some information from them."

Sophie's nerves spiked. "Are you sure about this? A lot of us will die."

"I know but it has to be done. I just hope there will be enough of you left to help close the eternal flame for good."

"Alright, I'll keep you updated. Stay safe."

"I will."

Sophie stood from the table and searched for Liam. She hated that he was right but knew he needed all the help he could get. There was a lot depending on them and to Sophie that meant failure was not an option. When Sophie finally caught sight of Liam she rushed up to him, hoping for a polite conversation.

Liam took one look at Sophie's face, filled with fear and said, "I'm not calling this thing off."

"That's not why I'm here," she began. "I want to help."

This caught his attention. "Why? What happened?"

Sophie looked around, not wanting the wrong person to overhear their conversation. *"I talked to Lottie."*

Liam's eyes widened. *"What did she say?"*

"She wants this riot to happen. She's hoping we can get some information about what they're planning here."

"Their army will be too busy handling us to be able to focus on shielding the minds of the people running this place. It's brilliant."

"What can I do to help?" Sophie finally asked aloud.

"The plan needs to change slightly," Liam answered. "I need you to get people who are willing to follow the guards and other employees so their minds can be read immediately."

Sophie nodded and made her way towards groups of people she knew Liam couldn't get to agree to his plan. She knew it wouldn't be easy convincing them to do something so dangerous but it was a lot harder than she imagined. They were all committed to

103

the previous plan and didn't want to risk their lives further.

Liam watched as she struggled. He wondered if she would be able to convince even a single person. He considered helping her but wanted her to succeed on her own. He planned to step in if he absolutely needed to.

After a while, Sophie seemed to be doing pretty well. "I managed to convince some people to do what we talked about. They just need to know when."

Chapter 17

"Things are not looking good right now," Lottie said as she looked out the window.

The new safe house was a rundown farmhouse they came across while driving down the highway. Tim parked the car a couple of miles away in case anyone went looking for it.

"Did something happen?" Tim asked.

Lottie didn't want to let Tim know everything that was going on. It would only worry him more. She definitely didn't trust Mary enough to let her in on anything. Lottie wasn't happy about having to bring Tim and his family along to the new safe house. Matt wouldn't let her leave them behind. It would have weighed too heavily on his conscience.

"Lottie, what is it?" Matt asked.

She couldn't risk the others hearing the conversation. *"Things are worse than I thought. They're keeping secrets at the facility."*

"What kind of secrets?"

"I don't know yet but if they're using their psychic soldiers to protect the thoughts of everyone working there, they're planning something."

"Whatever they're up to is not going to end well if we can't find out what it is. Do you have any ideas how we can get information?"

"I've got Liam and Sophie on it."

"Are you guys going to tell us what's happening or just stare longingly into each other's eyes?" Mary asked, clearly irritated.

"They weren't just staring at each other, Mary," Tim clarified. "They were having a telepathic conversation."

Confusion showed on Mary's face. "What? That's impossible."

"I don't care if you believe it or not," Lottie snapped. "You just worry about yourself. You don't need to know anything about what's going on."

"Lottie," Matt whispered.

"No, I'm not going to sit here and pretend she isn't a threat to us!" Lottie shouted. "We were held against our will for five years and she has no idea what that's like. She's never going to be useful to us."

Matt pulled her in for a hug. "Lottie, you don't mean any of that, you're just upset."

Tim turned to Lottie. "She didn't mean anything by it. She just doesn't know about any of this stuff. I didn't believe in any of it either until I started working at the facility."

Lottie glared at Mary. "We don't have time to explain any of this to her."

"You won't have to," Tim replied. "I'll explain everything to her and we won't have a problem. It'll be fine."

"You don't even know half of what went on in there," Lottie argued.

"Lottie, you're not helping," Matt said, trying to calm her down.

She took a deep breath. She didn't know what had been going on with her. Was it just stress and fear of the situation or was there something more happening? Either way, Lottie didn't have the time to stop and try to figure herself out.

"Now that we're in this new house, let's try to keep it a secret," Lottie began. "It's not good for the kids to have to move from home to home like this."

She was clearly aiming her words at Mary who had informed the police of their situation. The tension between those two was so thick that it made everyone else uncomfortable. The two women clearly had different upbringings and different ideas of what made good parenting.

Mary, with her dark brown hair tightly coiled in a bun, pale complexion and ice blue eyes was straight laced and wound just as tightly as her hair. She judged Lottie harshly for being a mother at such a young age. She assumed she was reckless and a bad mother.

Lottie, being able to read Mary's thoughts, knew all of this. She didn't want to waste any of her time explaining to Mary all that she'd been through. She deemed Mary unworthy of her time. All Lottie cared about was surviving the nightmare with her family intact.

Mary looked down, feeling guilty about what she did. Had she known just how dangerous the situation was, she never would have told anyone where they were. But she wanted answers; she deserved to know what kind of danger her family was in. She was tired of being treated like dirt by Lottie.

"Can you please just keep me informed about what's going on?" Mary asked as calmly as she could manage.

"I suppose I could try," Lottie replied coldly.

"What exactly did you go through in there?" she asked.

"No," Lottie snapped. "You don't get to know about all of that."

She rushed out of the room without waiting for anyone else to tell her she was being rude. She didn't want to hear it. Matt rushed to make sure she was alright. He knew something was going on with her.

109

"Lottie what has been going on with you?"

"I don't know, Matt," she cried. "Is there something wrong with me?"

"Mommy," Emma said as she came into view. "You have two heartbeats."

Lottie looked at her daughter with confusion. "What? No Emma, that's not possible."

"But you do," Emma insisted. "One up here and one down here."

"Are you sure about this, Emma?" Matt asked.

Emma hugged her parents. "I'm going to have a baby brother!"

Matt and Lottie could only stare at each other. Not a single thought passed between the two. Only shock existed in the air. It was the worst time possible for them to have another baby.

Chapter 18

Only the emergency lights were on in the entire facility, giving an ominous look to the already depressing atmosphere. Sophie ran for cover from the soldiers. All she could think about was making it through the riot alive. She had to. She thought she would be safe under the table in an interrogation room. That's where she was headed when the riot started.

Liam on the other hand was thoroughly enjoying the chaos. He wanted to do this since day one. Lottie always told him to be patient and wait for the right moment. He thought about her as he caused maximum chaos, it was all for Lottie.

The soldiers stormed the place the second the riot began. It was like they knew it was coming but they wanted to wait until everyone was out in the open. Many prisoners died in the first couple of minutes. It was more of a massacre than anything else.

As terrified as Sophie was, she knew she had a job to do. She needed to leave her hiding spot and go get some information. Lottie wanted her to follow one person, Jay. Her search for him didn't last long and she didn't need to get very close to be able to read his mind. Once she located his thoughts, Sophie sought shelter in a ransacked office so she wouldn't be disturbed.

She poked around his thoughts and memorized every idea that ever crossed his mind and every conversation he ever had. She was sure something in there would be useful to them. Seconds seems like hours to Sophie who could still hear all of the chaos going on outside the office. She shook more and more violently with each passing moment no matter how hard she tried to focus on her job.

"Liam, where are you?"

"I'm in the cafeteria, did you find out what they're planning?"

"I did. I'm on my way to you now."

Sophie carefully made her way towards the cafeteria. Her breathing loud and keeping pace with each step she took. Gasps escaped her each time she rushed to hide from a soldier or guard. Her only thought was to make it through the riot alive.

"Sophie, over here," Liam called the second she was in sight.

Sophie stared in horror at the sight of the dozens of dead bodies scattered around the room. Tables were overturned and there was food all over the floor. The worst part for her was the stench of blood that filled her nose.

"Can we go somewhere safe?" she asked.

"Nowhere is completely safe around here."

"I'm just not comfortable being out in the open like this."

Liam sighed. "Alright, let's go to the cells."

He took one last longing look back at the chaotic fighting before following Sophie to her cell. The second they set foot inside, the door automatically shut.

Sophie struggled with the locked door. "What just happened?"

"I figured this would happen," Liam said as he plopped down on Sophie's bed. "So, what is it that Jay has planned?"

"You really want to talk about this right now? We're trapped in here!"

"We're already in a prison, how is being locked in a cell any different?"

"We have to get out of here!" Sophie panicked.

"I don't think that's going to happen anytime soon. You wanted to be someplace safe, now here we are."

"You don't understand, Liam! They're going to kill us all!"

Liam put a hand over his mouth as he thought. "Weren't they always going to kill us if we didn't prove useful to them?"

"This is different," Sophie began. "After Matt and Lottie escaped with Emma, they decided to get rid of the entire facility; every one of us dead so they can start over completely."

Liam's heart sank. "Do you have any idea how many of us have already died? We just made it easier for them."

"We have to get out of here."

"How? It's not like we can leave the same way Matt and Lottie did."

"I don't know but if we don't find a way to escape, we're going to die and everything they're doing out there will be for nothing."

Panic set in for the pair as that thought sank in.

Chapter 19

Tim walked in the room and instantly noticed Matt and Lottie's worried expressions. "Do we have to leave again?"

Still unable to fully process the news, Lottie shook her head.

"No," Matt answered, struggling to keep his composure.

"Then what's wrong?"

"I think I'm pregnant," Lottie said quietly.

Tim tilted his head. He didn't hear her. "What?"

"I'm going to have a baby brother!" Emma beamed with excitement.

Tim looked at Matt then Lottie in disbelief. "Is this true?"

"We need a doctor to confirm it but we're pretty sure," Matt replied.

"How can we see a doctor?" Lottie asked in a panic. "It'll point them in our direction immediately."

"I might know someone who can help," Tim offered. "I can make some calls."

"It's too dangerous."

"Lottie, you need help," Matt insisted.

"This stress isn't good for you either."

"This is the worst time possible for me to have another baby." She looked at Matt. "Can we even do this?"

He grabbed her hand. "It won't be easy...especially when you consider that we were sixteen when we were taken. We didn't even finish high school. We have no skills to help us function in the real world."

"You're not helping, Matt."

"Sorry."

Tim's eyes widened. "You guys were only *sixteen* when you were thrown in that place? I had no idea. What kind of monster would do such a thing?"

117

"Tim, call whoever you need to," Lottie ordered. "Just make sure no one can track us."

Tim nodded and left the room immediately.

"How are you feeling about this?" Matt asked, already half knowing the answer.

"I'm scared...I feel useless. How am I supposed to help in this fight against the eternal flame when I have another life to worry about?"

"You're not useless Lottie. You came up with this whole plan."

"Yeah but I was fully prepared to put myself in harm's way...that's not an option anymore."

"Don't worry about all of that, everything's going to work out."

Tim poked his head back into the room. "The doctor will be here in the morning."

"Thanks Tim," Matt and Lottie said at the same time.

"Lottie, we need help."

"Sophie? What's wrong?"

"The riot backfired on us. They're going to kill everyone in here. We're trapped."

Lottie's heart sank. "They need us."

"What is it?"

"I just heard from Sophie, she said that they're going to kill everyone in the eternal flame."

"We have to go back, mommy," Emma insisted.

"That's exactly what I was thinking," Lottie replied.

"You can't be serious!" Matt shouted. "You're pregnant, Emma's a child. We made it out! There's no reason for us to ever go back there!"

"Matt, we have to," Lottie calmly replied. "They *need* us."

"Sophie, we're coming to get you. Is Liam alive?"

"He's alive but Lottie, if you come back here, you might die with the rest of us."

"That's a risk I'm willing to take. I'm not letting this go any farther."

"What are you going to do?"

"We'll come up with a plan on the way, just make sure everyone left is gathered near an exit for a fast escape."

"I don't think I can do that. Liam and I are locked in my cell. We've been trying to get out for hours."

"Melt the lock. Trust me, it'll work."

"Lottie, you should stay here with Emma," Matt suggested. "If anyone's going anywhere, it should be me and Tim."

"You were just telling me that I'm not useless so let me do this."

"What about Emma?"

"She can help, she wants to help."

"But if anything happens to her…" Matt trailed off, unable to bring himself to think of the horrible possibility.

"Daddy, I can help. I've seen it," Emma said.

"Can you show us what you saw?" Lottie asked.

Emma placed one hand on Matt's face and the other on Lottie's as she sent the vision to her parents. The smell of blood lingered in the air. Dead bodies scattered in every direction. Emma ran through the halls of the facility with Matt and Lottie as if she had a shield of invisibility surrounding the three of them.

Without looking at the rest of the vision, Matt looked at Lottie and back at Emma. "Are you sure you're able to do that?"

"Yes, daddy," Emma answered. "I'm just not sure I can do it with so many people at once."

"Matt we have to do this."

Matt shook his head. "I really don't like this, but you're right."

Lottie went into the next room where Tim was enjoying time with his family. "Tim, we need your help."

"What is it?"

"We have to go back to the facility. We need one big military vehicle. And you're the only one who knows how to get there."

"He's the only one of us who knows how to drive, Lottie."

"That too, but that's not the point. We need to leave...right now."

"Can you back up a second?" Tim asked, frazzled. "Why do we *have* to go back there?"

"Everyone's being murdered as we speak," Lottie explained. "Come on, we have to go!"

Tim grabbed his shoes and coat as Matt and Lottie rushed him towards the door. "Hang on a second," he said, looking at Emma. "She can't come with us."

"She has to," Matt insisted. "I don't like it either but we need her."

"You can't be serious!" Mary shouted. "She's staying with me."

"Mary, back off!" Lottie yelled. "This isn't your decision."

Mary immediately felt ashamed and sat back down.

"We need to hurry," Matt said as he helped Emma out the door.

Chapter 20

"Thank God it worked!" Liam exclaimed.

"We have to help the others get out. Where should we gather them?"

"Knowing Matt and Lottie, they would come in the same way they left. I say we gather everyone over there."

"Wouldn't that be where the most soldiers gather?"

Liam groaned. "You're probably right. But we need to get as close to there as possible. I just know that's where they'll be coming in."

"So let's start by looking around for a safe place to gather everyone," Sophie suggested.

They made their way towards the vehicles, stumbling over dead bodies along the way. As much as Sophie didn't want to cry, the scene brought tears to her eyes. She could still hear shouting from the soldiers and surviving prisoners.

Liam seemed to enjoy the riot a lot less than he did when it started. As he looked down at the lifeless bodies of his friends, he was reminded of the fact that he could be next. It fueled the fire in him to shut the place down. All he needed to do was make it out alive.

"There are too many soldiers around here," Sophie whispered. "We'll never make it close enough to the vehicles."

"Let's find a room down here to hide in," Liam said as he pointed down the hallway.

They walked down the hall and into various training rooms. There was enough space for a decent amount of people. They weren't sure if they would be safe from the soldiers in those rooms but they knew how important it was for them to take the risk. They wordlessly agreed on the gathering spot and left to find as many survivors as they could.

"Do you think there are many of us left?" Sophie asked.

"I don't know." Liam felt his nerves starting to get the better of him. "I don't have a good feeling about it."

"There are so many people here dead already. How do we know we're not the last two survivors?"

That thought hadn't occurred to Liam. "It has gone pretty quiet around here. Maybe we should check the cells. If we got locked in, I'm sure others did too."

"Let's hope they're still alive."

"Sophie, are you alright in there?"

"Lottie, I'm glad to hear your voice. I'm still alive but things could be better."

"I'm on my way. We're going to get you guys out of there. Do you have a lot of people ready to leave?"

"Liam and I are having some trouble finding survivors."

"Keep looking, we'll let you know when we're close."

"I just heard from Lottie, she's on her way."

"That's a relief. What is she going to do when she gets here?"

"I'm not sure, she just said she'll let me know when she's close."

Liam let out a small chuckle. "She must not have a plan yet."

"Why would she rush here without a plan?"

"She heard that we're in trouble and knew it was better to get here as fast as possible," he explained. "Lottie's great at making up plans as she goes."

"What do you think she's going to do once she gets here?"

"She'll get as many of us out as she can. After that, who knows what she has up her sleeves."

"What does that mean?"

"I'm saying that Lottie can see all possible outcomes of a situation at any given moment. She never needs to spend much time thinking about a plan because as a situation unfolds, she adapts."

"There aren't many people in the cells," Sophie pointed out.

"Some is better than none. We have to get them out."

Liam quickly got to work on melting all of the locks. Sophie tried helping but could barely manage creating a spark. Sophie led a group to the agreed upon gathering spot as Liam continued letting everyone out of the cells.

Sophie wasn't prepared to fight the soldiers who stood in the way. She was frozen in fear as the other prisoners put up a fight. She watched as some of the group died. One soldier locked eyes with her and she felt paralyzed. That was when she felt the heat within her rise. The searing pain was quickly expelled in an explosion that instantly killed everyone around her.

"Oh God," she whispered. "What did I do?"

Crying and in shock, she rushed back to find Liam. She had no clue how she was going to explain to him what happened, she wasn't even sure about what happened herself.

"Sophie, you look awful..."

"Liam...something happened," she interrupted. "I don't know exactly what it was but I exploded and now everyone who was there is dead."

He didn't know how to process the information. He didn't fully understand what she was telling him and he wasn't sure he ever would. "Even the innocent ones are dead?"

Sophie felt ashamed of herself. "Yeah."

Liam took a deep breath. "Well, we have to keep moving forward."

They found as many survivors as they could and took them towards the rooms they agreed on earlier. There seemed to have been more soldiers closing in on them as they went along. Sophie was too scared of killing everyone in the room so she hid while everyone else fought their way through.

"Is it just me or does it seem like they're trying to corner us?" Sophie asked as she came out of hiding once the soldiers left.

"Something's not right," Liam agreed. "It's like they're trying to lead us somewhere else."

"Yeah, but where?"

"I have no idea."

"How are you doing Sophie? We're coming in."

"I'm alive. Where are you?"

"We're close."

Sophie breathed a sigh of relief. "They're here."

"Thank God," Liam whispered. "Where are they?"

"Right behind you Liam," Lottie answered.

Liam threw his arms around Lottie. "I'm so glad you guys are here."

"Can't say the same," Matt said. "Let's focus on getting everyone out of here."

Liam looked down at Emma. "Why did you bring Emma with you?"

"You'll see," Lottie answered. "Is this everyone you could find."

"Yes," Sophie replied.

"It'll have to do," Matt remarked.

"They're coming," Sophie panicked. "What are we going to do?"

Matt put a hand on her shoulder. "Relax, we've got it covered."

"Alright Emma, just like we practiced," Lottie said.

Suddenly the soldiers rushed into the room. The confused expressions on their faces were apparent when they slowly walked through looking for signs of someone. They heard some of the soldiers mumble about swearing someone was in the room as they walked back out.

Terror turned to relief the second the soldiers were out of sight. Everyone could finally stop holding their breath. Though they didn't quite understand how the soldiers couldn't tell they were standing in the middle of the room. Matt and Lottie were the only ones who felt no fear, only pride for their daughter.

"What was that?" Liam finally asked.

"It's one of Emma's abilities," Matt explained. "We don't quite understand it yet but this is why we brought her with us."

"Matt, you take Emma and the rest of these guys out of here. I'm going to go grab the kids."

"Lottie you can't do it all on your own," Matt protested.

"Then I'll bring Sophie with me."

"How are you going to get back unseen? You're going to need Emma's help."

"Then you two come find me when everyone else is safe."

"Just take care of yourself Lottie. I don't want anything to happen to you."

Lottie bent down and gave Emma a kiss. "You be safe, okay?"

"I will mommy."

Lottie and Sophie watched as everyone disappeared right in front of them. She knew they would make it out alive.

"Let's hurry up," Lottie ordered.

"Why are we doing this?"

"You have no idea how many children are here. They don't deserve to be trapped."

"I never thought about that."

"That's because you weren't here very long."

"I guess there's a lot I didn't get to learn about this place."

"Consider yourself lucky, Sophie. If you knew everything that went on in here, you would want to torch the place."

"I might be able to," she mumbled.

Even though Lottie could barely hear what she said, she saw Sophie's memory of what happened. "You really could torch the place."

Her eyes widened in shock. "Did Liam tell you what happened?"

"No, I just saw your memory. It's not your fault."

"But I killed all of those people. Some of them were innocent."

"Some of them weren't."

"Is that supposed to make me feel better?"

"No," Lottie answered. "You haven't learned how to control this ability yet. Don't beat yourself up about it."

"So what happens now?"

"We're almost at the nursery so we're going to take as many babies as we can to safety."

The closer Lottie got to the door, the more anxious she became. She had a feeling there was something awful on the other side. But she had to save those babies; she had to at least try.

The smell was the first thing they noticed when the door opened. Decay. Lottie's eyes filled with tears as she entered the room and saw the true horror of the situation. Sophie couldn't enter the room once the smell reached her nose.

"They killed all of the babies," Lottie sobbed. "They didn't deserve this."

A thought occurred to Lottie and she ran out of the room and down the hall. Sophie couldn't bear to follow. It was as though she already knew what was coming. She heard Lottie running from room to room and began to cry.

"They're all dead...aren't they?" Sophie asked when Lottie finished her search.

"Every single one."

Great sadness filled the air as the pair stood there in a moment of silence for the hundreds of children lost in the senseless massacre. All that could be heard was the sound of their sniffles.

Sophie wiped her tears and finally broke the silence. "We should probably get out of here."

Lottie gasped. "Emma."

"What about her?"

"Matt don't come over here. We're on our way back."

"Why? Don't you need help with the kids?"

"They were all killed. I don't want Emma to see that."

"Alright Lottie, be careful."

Lottie turned to Sophie. "I just told them not to come. Emma shouldn't have to see that."

"Good thinking." She paused for a moment, not wanting to ask her question. But her curiosity got the best of her. "How did you and Matt end up having Emma?"

The question caught Lottie off guard. "Don't you know where babies come from?"

"Yeah I know about all of that but I mean...never mind. It sounds bad no matter how I ask."

Lottie quickly understood what Sophie was really trying to ask. "The strongest of us were paired off and forced into relationships."

"So you were forced to...do that?"

"Yeah." Lottie seemed to be staring blankly as the memories of what happened to her flooded back in her brain. "You'd be surprised at what you're willing to do when your life is threatened."

"I had no idea."

"You're lucky you didn't have to go through all of that."

"Hey are you guys okay?" Liam asked as they left the building.

They had been so consumed by what happened that they didn't realize they were moving so quickly. Their eyes were puffy and red from all of the crying. Lottie wondered if Matt had explained what happened to everyone else but judging by Liam's question, he clearly didn't. Neither of them wanted to talk about what they experienced. They just wanted to forget.

"Hang on," Lottie said. "This place needs to burn."

Liam and Lottie both stared at Sophie.

"No, I shouldn't do it. I could accidentally kill all of you."

"You won't," Lottie assured. "You can control it."

"But what happens if I can't?"

"We all die," Liam answered.

Lottie hit him on the back of the head. "Not helping, Liam."

Everyone watched in anticipation as Sophie turned to face the building. She wasn't sure how she exploded the first time and didn't know what to do to repeat it. A lot was depending on her ability to do this one thing.

Her heart raced with anxiety. The more she thought about what she was trying to do, the worse she felt. That anxiety built until she couldn't take it anymore. She let out a scream and along with it, an explosion. Another blast escaped as she realized she wasn't able to control it.

"Oh no, not again," Sophie cried.

When the flames finally subsided Sophie turned around, expecting to see the dead bodies of her friends. To her surprise, they were all alive and well. She gazed at them through a blue protective shield as it burst like a bubble.

"Did the baby do that?" Matt asked.

"I think so," Lottie answered in shock.

Everyone stared at Lottie, unsure about what to make of the situation. They were all grateful she was able to protect them but they didn't know how it was possible. The biggest shock of the whole thing was the news that Lottie was going to have another baby.

"You're pregnant?" Liam asked as they climbed into the back of the truck.

"I think it's safe to say yes," Matt answered with a laugh.

"I was going to say that we need to have it confirmed by a doctor but that shield wasn't mine," Lottie added.

"I know," Liam began. "Yours is purple. But what I'm wondering is how your baby was able to do that."

"I'm wondering the same thing," Lottie replied.

"So where are we going?" Sophie asked as the truck started moving.

Matt and Lottie glanced at each other. They knew the truth wasn't ideal but it was all they could come up with on such short notice. Liam had spent enough time with them to know that something was up so he read their minds.

"Oh really?" he shouted. "You couldn't come up with something better?"

"We know living in an abandoned warehouse isn't ideal but it was all we could come up with in such a short amount of time," Matt explained.

"I don't think we'll be there very long," Lottie added.

"What will we do once we get there?" Sophie asked.

"Now that the eternal flame is destroyed, we have to make sure they can't do this ever again," Matt answered. "We're going to make the public aware of the situation."

"Are you sure that's a good idea?" Liam asked. "You know what they do to threats."

"You can stay out of this if you're too afraid but I'm not going to let this happen all over again," Lottie declared.

Liam sighed. "Who are we talking to first?"

"Lottie and I were thinking it would make à good impact if we made sure the military was aware of this first."

"If they try to keep this quiet, we'll go to the media," Lottie added.

"I think the military is responsible for all of this in the first place," Liam stated. "How do you know they'll listen?"

"We don't," Lottie answered. "The truth is we don't know who is truly behind everything that went on inside the eternal flame."

"They could have been recruiting for a private military for all we know," Matt said. "As much as we've all been through in that place, there's still so much we don't know about it."

Chapter 21

"I just got a call from Mary," Tim started. "She said the explosion is being reported on the news."

"Are you sure it's the eternal flame?" Lottie asked. "It could easily be some other building they're talking about."

"She doesn't know anything about the facility so one of us will have to confirm it."

"We don't exactly have a TV in this place," Liam pointed out.

"Go find out if it's the eternal flame they're talking about," Matt ordered. "Lottie, Emma and I will help everyone get settled here."

"I'll be back as soon as I can."

Tim rushed back to his family hoping for some good news. He knew that if the media reported the explosion at the facility it meant less work they had to do. The whole situation could be over much sooner than he previously thought. It was all the hope he needed to help him make it through.

He wasn't cut out for being a fugitive. He didn't want his family to have to stay in hiding much longer. He so desperately wanted to go back to his old life; back before he was recruited to do interrogations in the facility. Things were simpler then, he didn't have to worry about him and his family getting murdered. He was carefree.

When he finally reached the safe house he saw the door was slightly open. He knew Mary never would have left it open no matter what. His heart raced as he thought of what might be waiting for him inside.

"Mary?" he called out as he carefully entered the house.

There was no response, only the sound of the news coming from the TV in the living room. His breathing got heavier as he made his way into the living room. His heart dropped when his wife and kids came into view. From behind it looked like they were all sitting on the couch watching TV. But when Tim saw them from the front, he saw bullet holes in each of their temples.

He dropped to the ground and cried. He lost track of time and completely forgot about what he was supposed to do. He was stuck in his own despair until Lottie's voice in his head snapped him out of it.

"Tim, I'm so sorry about your family."

"How do you know what happened?" he asked aloud.

"Remote viewing, I can see you right now. You have to snap out of it, they're coming for you."

"Let them come."

"Don't you want to get revenge on the people who did this to them? You can't do that if you're dead."

Tim picked himself up off the floor, took one last look at his family and rushed out the door. "What do I do now?"

"You can't come here. They're most likely going to have you followed."

"Then where am I supposed to go?"

"Head towards the facility, I doubt they'll be anywhere near there."

"What about the fire and news crews?"

"We'll meet somewhere along the way."

"That town where I picked you and Matt up."

"It'll have to do."

"See you there."

Chapter 22

"How did you get here?" Tim asked. "I thought you couldn't drive."

"Liam drove me," Lottie answered.

"Is he still around?"

"No, it's just me. I thought it would be safer this way."

"You're probably right."

An awkward silence fell over them for a moment. Neither of them knew what to say. They had both seen so much tragedy at the hands of the eternal flame. They were both determined to make them pay for their crimes.

"I think we should take this to the media," Lottie said, finally breaking the silence.

"I'll do whatever it takes to hurt them the way they hurt me."

They heard a recognizable voice coming from behind them. "I don't think either of you will be doing much of anything."

They turned around to confirm Jay's presence. He stood there with a smug look on his face. Confident that he had them beat, he pointed a gun at the two of them. That was when Lottie realized how much trouble they were in. Jay had them surrounded by soldiers.

"You wouldn't kill innocent people, would you, Jay?" Tim asked desperately.

Without hesitation, Jay pulled the trigger. One shot after the other, aimed at both Tim and Lottie. When he finally stopped to admire his work, he was surprised to see the pair standing there without a scratch. Then he noticed the shield.

"Your shield isn't blue, Charlotte. You're pregnant, aren't you?"

Lottie didn't bother answering.

"Then we can't kill you yet. You have valuable property within you."

"My baby is *not* your property!"

"But it is," he replied. "You see, that baby was conceived within the walls of the facility. Meaning it's our property."

Lottie shook her head. She couldn't believe what she was hearing. She calculated all of the possible outcomes of the situation and decided her best option was to let Jay take her. Matt would come for her, she was certain he would stop at nothing to get her back.

"What do you want from me, Jay?" Lottie asked.

"Tell me where your friends are."

She laughed. "You know that's not going to happen."

"Then you'll have to come with us."

"Fine"

"Lottie, no," Tim protested.

"It's fine Tim. I'll be fine."

"Are you sure?" he asked hesitantly.

She nodded.

"Time to go, Charlotte."

As Lottie turned to leave with Jay, the sound of a gunshot made her jump. Jay grabbed her arm to get her to keep moving forward. Lottie couldn't help but look back. She gasped as she saw Tim's lifeless body on the ground. It was all up to her now.

"Matt, I need your help. Tim's dead and Jay is taking me away. I don't know where he's taking me yet."

Even telepathically, Matt's anger was apparent. *"Did he hurt you?"*

"He tried to kill me but the baby saved me. He won't hurt me now."

"But if he's around when the baby's born, he'll most likely kill you immediately."

"That's why you need to come help me. I can't let him take our baby away."

"I hope you don't think I'm stupid."

Lottie didn't respond.

"I know you're planning something. Otherwise you wouldn't have agreed to come with me so easily."

Jay stared at Lottie, expecting her to say something. But she just looked forward as she was forced into the back of a van.

"I see you're going back to your old ways."

Lottie closed her eyes. She knew she needed to stay calm for the sake of the baby. She hoped Jay would let his guard down enough to be able to get more information from him. Whether he knew it or not, he was going to help her bring down whoever was responsible for all of her pain.

After hours of driving, they finally pulled up in front of a mansion. Lottie knew the owner of this extravagant home was the person in charge of the program that allowed the facility to function. Jay helped her out of the van and escorted her inside.

"I'm leaving. You'll be in good hands here."

She looked up at the massive chandelier hanging above her head. She liked how it glittered in the sun. She didn't need to walk further into the house to see tons of valuable

151

pieces of art. It seemed more like a museum to her than someone's home.

"You must be Charlotte," a man said as he walked down the grand staircase.

Lottie tore her eyes away from the art to look at who spoke. She was slightly grossed out at how greasy his brown, slicked back hair was. His hazel eyes had a twinkle of childish mischief in them. She was still trying to decide if she wanted to speak. Until then, all she could do was stare and try to figure the man out.

"I'm Anthony." He reached to shake her hand but Lottie instinctively backed away. "I won't hurt you. Let me take you to your room."

She finally spoke as they headed upstairs. "So you're the man in charge."

"I am. This is my home. I hope you'll be happy here, Charlotte."

"Lottie."

"Lottie it is." He stopped in front of a door. "I know you probably have a lot of questions but for now I want you to get settled. We'll talk later."

She opened the door, already knowing exactly what was on the other side. It was a big upgrade from her cell in the eternal flame. The walls were a calming, pale green color. There was a queen size bed in one corner and a desk in another. The closet was fully stocked with clothes of all sizes and styles. A chilling reminder to Lottie that she wasn't the first one to live there. Still, it was a better living arrangement than she had ever experienced.

"Matt, are you alright?"

"Oh thank God Lottie, I was starting to think I would never hear from you again. I'm alright, just worried about you."

"They brought me to a mansion. The man in charge of the program responsible for everything we've been put through owns this place."

"Is he there?"

"He is. I met him briefly."

"Do you have any idea why he started this whole thing?"

"I'm not sure yet but I'm going to find out. His name is Anthony, that's all I know for now."

"Keep me updated."

"I will. How's Emma doing?"

"She misses you a lot, Lottie. But she knows we're going to get you back."

"Tell her I love her."

"I will."

A knock on the door startled Lottie. She saw it was Anthony on the other side. "You can come in Anthony."

"How did you know it was me?" he asked as he opened the door. "Oh right, you're special."

"I wouldn't call it that." She paused for a moment. "Was there something you wanted?"

"I thought we could talk."

"What happened to letting me get settled first?"

"You'll get used to this place over time," he answered. "But I have a lot of questions for you too."

"Like what?" Lottie asked.

"How did you get you powers?"

"They're not powers. It's just stuff I can do. I've been able to do them for as long as I can remember."

"So you were born that way."

"I guess so. Why did you create this program?"

"Such a big question," he said. "Are you sure you don't want me to build up to a big reveal?"

"I just want answers."

"Alright, I'll give them to you. You might want to sit down. It's kind of a long story."

Lottie sat down on the bed while Anthony situated the desk chair across from her. He gazed at her for a moment, almost unsure of whether or not he wanted to reveal his secrets. But he wanted to talk; he *needed* to

tell someone everything that had been
weighing on him for decades.

"My brother was like you," he began.
"He was so powerful."

"What happened to him?"

"I killed him."

Chapter 23

A lot of thoughts raced through Lottie's mind. She wanted to hear Anthony's story but she also wanted to get as far away from him as possible. It was a struggle for her, her need to stay safe and her need to make sure he couldn't put anyone through the same torture ever again.

"Oh no, now you're scared of me," Anthony whined. "But you don't understand. I had to do it."

"Why?"

"Because he was using his powers for evil."

"What exactly did he do?"

"When we were kids, Vic found out he had these super powers. He could do all sorts of things I thought were only possible in the movies. It was *so* cool. But then he thought his powers made him better than everyone else. He started being mean to me and my friends."

"That's awful."

"I wanted so badly to get powers like his. I tried hard to get them but they never came. Vic was always there to laugh at me every time I failed."

"And that made you feel worse."

"It did," he replied. "Then one day he took his torture too far. He killed my best friend. He thought it would be funny to set fire to his house...with my friend inside."

"Oh my God, I'm so sorry."

"You seem genuinely upset," Anthony said suspiciously. "Why do you care about what happened to my friend?"

"I didn't know him but I know that no one deserves to be treated that way."

"Vic's reign of terror went on for years before I was finally able to kill him. I spent that time learning everything I could about his powers. When I finally knew his weakness, I used it to my advantage and stabbed him repeatedly."

Anthony kept an eye on Lottie to gage her reaction. He needed to know if she was just as heartless as his big brother. His story worried Lottie and she didn't want to let it show just how scared she was. She couldn't seem to get a clear read on the man in front of her. That made him the biggest threat to her.

Lottie knew it was important to choose her words carefully. "So you got revenge for your best friend's death..."

"Yeah."

"How did that get you involved in all of this?"

"After I killed Vic, his friends came after me."

"They wanted revenge."

He nodded. "They had powers like Vic. I thought my brother was the only one."

"So once you found out there were more, you wanted to study them."

"I wanted to make sure you guys couldn't hurt anyone ever again."

"Anthony, I'm not like them. Some of us are good people."

"I'm not willing to let the bad ones get away just because of a few good people."

"You must know nothing about what happened in the eternal flame."

"What's the eternal flame?" he asked, intrigued.

"That facility where you sent people like me...those of us held prisoner there call it the eternal flame."

"Why call it that?"

"The eternal flame is known as the destroyer of all souls. Once a soul touches the flame, it's erased out of existence. Those of us who have been kidnapped and forced into that facility are never heard from again. We die in there, in one way or another."

"I guess that's a fitting name."

"Do you have any idea what I went through in that place?" Lottie asked, her voice wavering slightly as she tried to stay calm.

"I heard you're having a baby," Anthony cheerfully said in an attempt to change the subject.

"No, you don't get to change the subject. Let me show you what a day in the eternal flame looked like."

Lottie placed her hands on Anthony's face and sent him visions of everything she had to endure in the facility. He didn't want to see any of it but couldn't stop the visions from entering his mind. Tears streamed down his face.

"That was awful," he whispered. "Did you really live through it?"

"Every second."

"I gave them orders to find out as much as they could about you guys but I had no idea that's what they were doing all these years."

"How could you not know?" Lottie asked skeptically.

"I funded the program, gave them orders and stayed here waiting for reports."

"What were your goals with the program?"

Anthony sighed. "Like I said, I wanted to make sure you guys couldn't hurt anyone ever again. But when I found out that some of you are good, I thought I could use the good ones to help do some good in the world."

"That's why the military recruitment started."

"Yes, I thought the good ones would be happy to help protect the people of this country."

"But now you know that's not the way things played out."

"I didn't think they were recruiting the bad ones."

"The bad ones, as you call them, were the only ones ever willing to join your twisted army!"

"You shouldn't let yourself get so angry," Anthony calmly stated. "It's not good for your baby."

Lottie took a deep breath. "You're right, Anthony."

"Do you know what you're having?"

"I think it's a boy but it's too soon to tell."

"Is this your first?"

Lottie looked down. "It's my fourth pregnancy."

"So you have *three* kids now? You look so young."

"Only one was allowed to live," she cried. "They killed my first two babies because they weren't psychic."

"That's awful." He grabbed Lottie's hand. "You have to believe that I had no idea any of this was going on."

She pulled her hand away from his. "How am I supposed to believe you? You're the one responsible for all of the torture I went through."

"Look into my mind."

"I've been trying since I got here. You have someone protecting you."

"No one is helping me," Anthony explained. "I told you before I had tried to get powers like my brother. If you can't read my mind…I guess it's because my hard work paid off."

"I'm sure you're happy about that."

"Yeah, but right now I need you to trust me. So look into my mind and see that I'm not lying. You have my permission."

Lottie looked into Anthony's mind. All barriers were lifted and she was able to confirm his story about his brother. It made her sad to see how awful Vic was to Anthony and his friends. After everything, she could see that his intentions were pure.

"So you're telling me the truth," Lottie said when she finished. "Now that you know everything that went on in the eternal flame, what are you going to do?"

"The facility was destroyed. What more can I do?"

"I need to know that you're not going to let this happen ever again. Are there any other facilities open?"

"You saw into my mind, you know there aren't."

"What about this place? What is it for and why was I brought here?"

"First of all, this is my house. Second, you were brought here because you were the only survivor of the explosion at the facility. They said you were having a baby and had nowhere else to live."

"The explosion happened but I wasn't the only survivor. I have friends who escaped with me but I'm keeping them somewhere safe until their safety can be guaranteed."

"So my men have been lying to me."

"Why would they do that if they answer to you?"

"They must be up to something."

"If they're using powerful and awful psychics in their military then they're probably

looking to do some serious damage," Lottie
pointed out.

"How do we find out what they're up
to?"

"Jay was always the one in charge in the
eternal flame. Call him back and let's see what
he's up to."

Chapter 24

"Sophie, are you alright?"

"I'm here Lottie, how are you?"

"I'm alright. Listen, I need to know everything you know about what Jay has been planning."

"It turns out that the massacre at the facility was just the beginning. Jay saw how powerful the psychic army had become and decided to use them for his own personal gain."

Lottie felt her heart beating faster and faster. *"What's he trying to gain?"*

"Power...over the whole world."

"Could that even be possible?"

"I don't know but he's going to do everything he can to gain more and more power."

"This is horrible. We can't let it happen. Do you think this whole thing will be over if he were to die?"

"Honestly, I think someone else will take his place once he's gone."

"So we have to get rid of all of them."

"It seems that way."

"Lottie, I just got off the phone with Jay, he's coming over," Anthony said as he reentered the room.

"He wants power. He's using his psychic military to get it."

"How do you know this?"

"Mind reader."

"Oh...right."

A vision of Jay bringing his army to the mansion suddenly flooded Lottie's mind. The fight would end with Lottie and Anthony trapped inside the burning home. There was no way they could make it out alive the way she saw things play out.

"We're in trouble. Jay's bringing his army here."

"Why would he do that?"

"Maybe he wants whatever power you have," Lottie answered in a panic.

"Matt, I need you to bring everyone to this mansion now."

"Lottie you sound worried. What's going on?"

"Jay is on his way here with his army. We're going to die if we don't do something to stop him."

"I just got your location, we're leaving now. Should I bring Emma?"

"Yeah, she can help."

"See you soon."

"Help is on the way," Lottie told Anthony.

"Who's coming?"

"The rest of the survivors," she answered. "I just hope they get here before Jay does."

"What do we do now?"

"All we can do is wait for someone to show up."

"That sounds boring," Anthony whined.

"Are we really the only people in this entire mansion?"

"Yeah, I don't usually have guests."

"This place is so big, doesn't it get lonely?"

"Sometimes it does."

"I'm sorry Anthony...for everything you've been through in your life. No one should have to go through that."

He was shocked by Lottie's words. He never expected someone like her to be so nice. In his experience they were all awful people.

"I should be apologizing to you! Everything you've been through is because of me. Can you ever forgive me?"

She nodded. "I forgive you."

"How can you forgive me so easily?"

"I wasn't going to but then you told me your story," Lottie explained. "I wouldn't have done things the same way but now I understand why things happened the way they did."

"You're such a good person. I wasn't expecting that."

"People can surprise you if you give them a chance."

Chapter 25

"Matt, I'm so glad you're here," Lottie exclaimed as she rushed to hug him.

Matt smiled. "You knew I was coming for you."

"This is Anthony, he owns the place," she said as she motioned towards Anthony.

He gave Matt a weak smile, clearly uncomfortable with the situation. He watched nervously as the rest of the survivors entered his home. It was better than certain death so he decided to try to be alright with everything going on around him.

"Is this whole thing really about to be over?" Liam asked.

"As long as we don't let anyone get away," Lottie answered.

"You're talking about killing all those people," Sophie started.

"You saw the people they killed," Lottie interrupted. "Consider it karma coming back for them."

"They could be here at any moment," Matt pointed out. "We should get ready for them."

Suddenly the lights cut out.

Liam just couldn't help himself. "They're here."

"Everyone get ready!" Lottie shouted.

"Emma, stay close to your mom and I."

She nodded and grabbed Lottie's hand.

Anxiety was high as everyone waited for the most important fight they ever had to face. Anthony ran to his hiding spot. He knew there wasn't much he could do and wasn't willing to risk his life.

Lottie could see they had the mansion surrounded. "A bunch of you need to make it outside."

The door burst open and the fight began. Jay was the first to die. The look on his face just before he died suggested that he didn't expect anyone to show up and fight. The first few soldiers to enter the mansion through the front door were the easiest to kill. The rest of them knew what was waiting for them inside and made it harder to be killed.

Matt, Lottie and Emma all fought next to each other as a family. Even at such a young age, Emma proved herself to be more talented than most psychics Lottie's age. Lottie stole every moment possible to make sure her daughter was alright. She was proud to see her deflect attacks with ease.

It was too easy to tell who was fighting for which side. The soldiers were all wearing protective gear while the survivors of the eternal flame were all dirty and dressed in tattered clothing. They were at a clear disadvantage with their only weapons being the psychic abilities they were able to develop while the soldiers had various guns.

"That must be Sophie," Lottie assumed as she heard the explosion.

"Hopefully she took a lot of them out," Matt added.

The ceiling above them collapsed. Lottie grabbed Emma and rushed out of the way. The house was on fire, meaning the fight had to be taken outside. The soldiers had them mostly surrounded, making it nearly impossible for them to get out.

Lottie suddenly felt a pulse come from within her. She knew it was her baby trying to help. The pulse grew stronger and stronger until it was finally able to escape in a blast of blue fire that killed every soldier blocking their exit. They were finally able to get outside and take care of the dozen remaining soldiers.

Low on ammo and outnumbered, the soldiers were finally afraid of defeat. One by one the life was swatted out of them like flies until there was only one left. Lottie looked into the soldier's mind to make sure there would be no one else to take over once he was dead.

Liam looked over, eager to make the kill that would end their suffering once and for all. Lottie nodded and Liam placed a hand on top of the soldier's head, melting it until only the skull remained. It was gruesome for them to watch but they were relieved to know that it was all over.

"Did Anthony make it out?" Lottie asked.

"No, he died in the blast," Sophie answered.

Lottie remotely viewed his body to be certain. She had mixed feelings about Anthony's death. Part of her was happy to be rid of him because he was responsible for everything she went through but knowing his story made it harder for her to enjoy the victory.

Lottie turned to the group. "Let's get out of here. It's all over now."

Chapter 26

"It's still hard to believe that this whole thing is over," Matt said. "And we didn't lose a single person during that fight."

"I know, it's crazy," Lottie replied. "Everyone's going back home to their family; I never thought I would live to see this day."

Matt held Lottie and Emma in his arms as he watched the rest of the group celebrate their freedom. The sight brought tears to Lottie's eyes.

"Why are you crying mommy?"

"I'm just really happy, Ems."

"Me too," she agreed.

The celebration didn't end until the early morning hours. Everyone except Matt and Lottie were asleep in the warehouse. Lottie enjoyed watching Emma sleep peacefully without having to worry about being separated from her.

"We should start tracking down everyone's families," Matt whispered.

Lottie nodded. "It's going to take a while to get everyone home. We may as well start now."

"I'm going to miss them."

"Me too but we can keep in touch with them if they want to."

"Telepathy has to be good for something," Matt laughed.

Matt and Lottie personally made sure everyone made it home safely. Tracking down all of those families and traveling across the country was no easy task but it was worth it to them to see the happy reunions. After everyone else was gone, Matt and Lottie realized they had decisions to make.

"Where are we going to live?" Lottie asked.

"Our families don't live too far away from each other, we could find someplace in the middle," Matt suggested.

"I'm kind of scared to go back."

"Why?"

"Because," Lottie began. "It's been five years and I have a daughter now and a son on the way. What if they don't want anything to do with us?"

"It's been five years. They'll be thrilled just to know you're alive. I think you owe them that much."

"Will you come with me?"

"Only if you meet my family too."

"Deal."

Lottie's stomach started doing flips as she thought more about what it meant to be going home.

"What's wrong?"

"It's just that…" Lottie sighed. "How are we going to survive in the real world now?"

"We'll figure it out."

Emotions were high as Matt and Lottie reunited with their families. Even Emma cried as she met her grandparents. To Lottie's relief, her parents were accepting of the new family members. But they insisted on meeting Matt's parents. The two families got along well and had a close bond.

Lottie insisted on getting a house off the grid where she didn't have to worry about having to function in society. Matt insisted on building the house himself so his father helped him build a stone house in the woods. It was nothing fancy, just big enough for Matt, Lottie and their two children.

It wasn't long before they were able to move in. Lottie's parents bought furniture for them while Matt's parents bought food and other essentials. Lottie quickly got to work on creating a beautiful garden in the back yard despite everyone else insisting she take it easy.

She watched as Matt chased Emma around the yard. Their laughter was a welcome treat, something she hadn't heard during her five years as a prisoner in the eternal flame. She was thrilled to finally have her freedom, they all were.

The End

About the author

Yvi Valentin is a poet and novelist from Chicago. Born with a creative spirit, she has spent most of her life writing. Her experiences with the paranormal inspired her to incorporate them into her novels.

For more information visit:

www.supposedlyspiritual.com

Made in the USA
Las Vegas, NV
26 January 2021

16596400R00111